WITCH
Chocolate
FUDGE

BEWITCHED BY CHOCOLATE
MYSTERIES

BOOK TWO

H.Y. HANNA

DEDICATION

To my husband, who is a wizard
with wit and words.

CONTENTS

CHAPTER ONE

There are a lot of things you can do when you're a witch but even magic can't control the English weather.

Caitlyn Le Fey glanced at the darkening sky above and quickened her steps, her breath coming faster as she climbed with greater speed up the hill. It had been raining non-stop all day—great torrents of water more suited to the tropics than to the Cotswolds countryside—but when the skies had finally brightened late afternoon and the downpour had stopped, she had thought that it was safe enough to venture out. It wasn't a long walk from the village of Tillyhenge to Huntingdon Manor, especially if you took the shortcut over the hill. She had been sure that she could get there in time to stay dry, even if the heavens did decide to open up

1

again.

But she should have known better than to underestimate the English weather. It was no wonder the British were so obsessed with it. It dominated people's lives and no one was exempt. *Not even if you're a witch*, thought Caitlyn with a wry smile.

Then she shook her head and laughed out loud. Barely a week ago, if someone had mentioned the word "witch" to her, never mind told her that she *was* one, she would have rolled her eyes in disbelief and amusement. Now? Well, after a week in Tillyhenge, magic and witchcraft didn't seem so impossible—or incredible—any more.

Something fell on the back of her neck, breaking into her thoughts. She reached up and touched the spot, feeling moisture on her fingers. A minute later, she felt a splatter on her face. Raindrops.

"Rats!" she muttered.

She looked ahead: she was almost at the top now—only a few more minutes of climbing and she would be standing on the crest of the hill—then she looked uncertainly over her shoulder, back the way she had come. The trail meandered back down the grassy slope and retraced her steps to the rear of the small stone cottage sitting at the edge of the village. She could still turn around. She could probably make it back into the cottage before the skies opened again.

Caitlyn hesitated, then turned resolutely

forwards and continued up the hill. No, she wasn't going to let a little rain deter her. She was already halfway there! If she turned back now, she would have walked twice the distance for nothing. Besides, Pomona would be so disappointed if she didn't visit as promised. Her cousin had had a pretty traumatic experience two days ago, after her romantic date had turned into a rendezvous with a cold-blooded murderer. And although she kept insisting that she was fine, Caitlyn was worried that Pomona was just putting on a brave face. She'd certainly seemed more subdued than usual when Caitlyn had visited her yesterday.

Reaching the top of the hill, Caitlyn heaved a breath and paused to look down the other side. The raindrops were starting to fall faster and heavier now, and in the distance she could see a sheet of rain moving diagonally across the landscape. It was heading her way. She started downhill, skidding slightly on the wet, muddy grass as she tried to hurry. The slope descended gently, levelling out to join the sprawling parkland which surrounded Huntingdon Manor—an elegant English country house in the Georgian style, with a sweeping front driveway and formal landscaped gardens, that was like something straight out of a Jane Austen novel.

And inhabited by a modern-day Mr Darcy too, thought Caitlyn with a slight blush. Well, if Mr Darcy smiled a lot more, had warm grey eyes, a charming manner, and a physique that any male model would have envied—not to mention a sexy British accent that left you weak at the knees. But Lord James Fitzroy, owner of Huntingdon Manor and the surrounding estates, including the village of Tillyhenge, was no clichéd "lord of the manor"—in fact, he combined aristocratic courtesy with a down-to-earth humility that had all his tenants in love with him, men as well as the ladies.

The rain was coming down in earnest now and Caitlyn started to run. She dashed across the manicured lawns edging the side of the Manor and headed for the closest door she could see. This was at the rear of the building—probably what used to be a service entrance for tradesmen—and she banged on it frantically as the rain pelted down around her. Hopefully one of the Manor staff would hear her and she'd have the chance to dry off before venturing into the main part of the house...

The door swung open and she looked up in dismay at the tall, handsome man framed in the doorway.

"Caitlyn!" James Fitzroy stared at her. "What on earth... you're soaked through! Come in, come in—" He grabbed her arm before she could protest and pulled her in out of the rain.

Caitlyn found herself standing in a dark hallway which obviously led into what used to be the old servants' quarters. She shivered as the water dripped off her and formed puddles on the floor.

"Here," said James, shrugging off his fine linen

jacket and draping it around her shoulders.

"Oh, no, it'll get wet! It'll be ruined—" Caitlyn protested.

James made an impatient sound. "Don't worry about it. The important thing is that you're warm."

"Th-thank you," said Caitlyn, wrapping the jacket around herself gratefully. It smelled of freshly laundered linen and a hint of expensive male aftershave.

James was looking at her in concern and she was suddenly terribly conscious of the fact that she probably resembled a drowned rat. She winced as she recalled their first meeting—she had thrown herself into a pond to rescue a drowning kitten and James had had to fish her out—that had ended with her all bedraggled and dripping wet too. She sighed. Why did she always have to meet him when she was looking her worst?

"Come on, we've got to get you some towels and a change of dry clothes..." James put a gentle hand under her elbow and began escorting her down the hallway, back towards the main part of the house.

"Oh, wait... I can't... I'll drip everywhere," protested Caitlyn, hanging back.

James raised an amused eyebrow. "I'm sure the floors can withstand a little water."

As she followed him reluctantly into the main part of the Manor, with its luxurious furnishings, priceless Aubusson carpets, and elegant chandeliers, Caitlyn felt even more self-conscious about her appearance. She had been so sure she'd have the time to make herself presentable, if she came in via the rear entrance—who would have thought that the master of Huntingdon Manor himself would open the door?

"I was looking for my housekeeper, Mrs Brixton," James said, as if in answer to her unspoken question. "And it's a good thing I was! Otherwise you might have been stuck out in the rain for ages because no one would have heard you knocking. Everyone is preoccupied preparing for the Summer Garden Party."

"The Summer Garden Party?"

"Didn't Pomona tell you? It's a Fitzroy family tradition. We hold a Summer Garden Party every year, a few days before the Summer Solstice, here on the Manor grounds. It's primarily for the tenants and villagers, although everyone is welcome, naturally," he added with a smile. "I hope to see you and Pomona there."

"Oh. Thanks." Caitlyn shyly returned his smile. "What usually happens at the party?"

James chuckled. "A lot of cake-eating and tea-drinking—what else? But in actual fact, I'm hoping to change things a little in the future. With my father's death last year, a lot of the villagers have been anxious about whether the old traditions might continue. I'd like to reassure them, but—since this is the first party where I'm stepping into the role of the host—I'd also like to introduce some new elements and liven things up a bit." He gave a rueful laugh. "It has required a lot of extra work and coordination, though, so I'm not sure the staff are all that pleased with me... Ah, Mrs Brixton!" He looked up as a middle-aged woman entered the hall from the other end and walked towards them.

Caitlyn's heart sank as the housekeeper approached. She had met Mrs Brixton briefly a few times before and she didn't like the woman. Tall and angular, with a pinched nose, calculating blue eyes, and a thin, almost lipless mouth, Mrs Brixton exuded all the arrogance and snobbery that her employer lacked. She even *looked* liked the stereotypical Victorian housekeeper, with her hair pulled back in a severe bun and an old-fashioned ring of keys that she always seemed to carry around with her.

"Yes, Lord Fitzroy?" said Mrs Brixton, eyeing Caitlyn with undisguised disgust as she took in the girl's wet, dishevelled appearance.

"I wondered if you could fetch some towels for Miss Le Fey and some of Miss Vanessa's clothes?" James turned to Caitlyn with a smile. "My sister lives in London but she keeps some things in her room here. I'm sure she wouldn't mind you borrowing a couple of items. In fact, would you like to have a hot shower in one of the guest rooms?"

"Oh, no!" said Caitlyn quickly. "Just some towels would be fine, honestly. And maybe just something to wear while my own clothes are drying—that

7

would be great."

"Mrs Brixton, if you would be so kind...?" James turned back to the other woman.

The housekeeper pressed her thin lips together. "I'll see what I can find, sir."

"Thank you," said James. He turned back to Caitlyn once more. "I need to return to my study—I'm awaiting a conference call—but Mrs Brixton will show you over to the private wing when you're ready."

As soon as James was out of earshot, Mrs Brixton turned to Caitlyn and said sourly, "You can change in the old servants' quarters. No need to go upstairs and get mud all over the carpets. And there's one of the maids' spare uniforms that you can wear while you're waiting."

Caitlyn flushed slightly at the woman's contemptuous manner but she did feel uncomfortable about tracking mud and dirt all over the Manor, not to mention borrowing James's sister's clothes, so she said nothing as she followed the housekeeper back to the rear of the house. A few minutes later, she was peeling her wet clothes off in a small bathroom at the end of the servants' corridor. She dried herself quickly with the towel provided and squeezed as much water as she could out of her hair, then contemplated the dress that Mrs Brixton had left for her.

It was a simple black maid's uniform, made of polyester, and looked about her size, although when

Caitlyn slipped it on, she was dismayed to find that it stretched tight across her hips and thighs in the most unflattering manner. Obviously it hadn't been designed for someone with the classic pear-shaped figure who needed a little extra room around her bottom! Caitlyn sighed. Well, beggars couldn't be choosers. She just hoped that her own clothes could be dried quickly.

Speaking of which... She picked up the wet bundle and stepped out of the bathroom, hesitating in the corridor. Mrs Brixton hadn't said anything about offering to dry her clothes but Caitlyn was determined not to let herself be intimidated by the other woman's insolent manner. She remembered that the housekeeper had a sitting-room-cum-office at the back of the house and she wandered slowly down the corridor, searching for it.

As she turned a corner, she spied a familiar oak cabinet and the sitting room door next to it. The door was slightly ajar. She hurried over and was about to knock when she froze with her hand raised. From inside the room came the sound of angry voices, followed by the *thwack* of something smacking down on a table.

"... don't you threaten me, Mrs Brixton, or I'll... I'll make sure you regret it!"

CHAPTER TWO

"Temper, Amelia. There's no need to get hysterical. I am simply offering you a business proposition: pay me a portion of your wages and keep your job, or I'll have you fired for stealing."

"That's not a business proposition—that's blackmail!"

Mrs Brixton laughed nastily. "You can call it whatever you like. As long as we understand each other."

"An' what if I go to Lord Fitzroy an' tell him what you're doin'? I bet he wouldn't be happy to find out that his housekeeper's an old slag who blackmails people!"

"I would deny everything," said Mrs Brixton calmly. "Who do you think he is going to believe? A silly maid who hasn't been working here six months? Or his respectable housekeeper who has been with the family for years?"

There was an uneasy silence. "I... I wasn't really stealin'. Not for myself, anyway."

"I'm sure that's what all the thieves say when they make off with the silver," said Mrs Brixton with another nasty laugh.

"No, this is different! An' anyway, Lord Fitzroy would never have even noticed."

"Well, he certainly won't if I don't tell him," Mrs Brixton purred. "But I will need something to ensure my silence. Oh, I'll give you some time to think it over. Shall we speak again after the Garden Party? You may go now, Amelia."

There was an angry silence, then footsteps hurried to the door and, before Caitlyn could pull back, the door was flung open and a girl rushed out. Caitlyn recognized her as one of the maids. The girl's face was a mask of fury, her eyes blazing, and she barely noticed Caitlyn as she stormed past and disappeared down the corridor.

Caitlyn hesitated, then knocked on the open door and stepped into the sitting room. It was a large space, handsomely furnished with a sofa, armchair, large desk, and several cabinets. Like the housekeeper herself, though, the room was quite severe in appearance. The walls and curtains were in sombre shades of grey and navy, and the few decorations were limited to a potted plant on the desk, a framed watercolour on one of the walls, and

11

a clock and a blue-and-white china jug on the mantelpiece.

Mrs Brixton was sitting at the desk. She looked up as Caitlyn came in.

Caitlyn held up the bundle in her hands. "Hello... here are my wet clothes."

The housekeeper's lips tightened. For a moment, Caitlyn almost felt like she should offer to find the dryer herself, then she bit her tongue. It wasn't that she expected to be waited upon but she didn't want to give this unpleasant woman the satisfaction of seeing her cowed.

"I would appreciate it if you could have them dried as quickly as possible, Mrs Brixton," she said pleasantly, walking over and placing the sodden bundle down next to the ring of keys on the woman's desk. "And Lord Fitzroy said you'd be able to show me over to the private wing?"

"I'm sure you can find the way yourself," said the housekeeper coldly. "I am very busy—especially now that I'll have extra work seeing to your wet clothes— and I really don't have the time to shepherd people around. Most of Lord Fitzroy's *usual* guests are familiar with these types of residences and wouldn't need help navigating their way around the Manor."

Caitlyn took a deep breath, trying not to let the woman's rudeness get to her. She didn't want to waste more time standing here or spend longer in the housekeeper's company than was necessary.

Giving the woman a breezy smile, she said,

"Thanks. You're right, I'm sure I'll find my way."

Her confidence was short-lived, however, when she found herself hopelessly lost several minutes later, wandering through vast drawing rooms with soaring ceilings and ornate hallways hung with oil paintings. She turned a corner and bumped into a group of Japanese tourists being given a guided tour, standing in the grand foyer with its sweeping Baroque staircase. Like many stately homes in England, Huntingdon Manor was too big now for its present-day owners and, after his father's death, James had decided to open up two thirds of the house to the public. In less than a year, it had gained a reputation as a top venue for weddings and events, as well as an ideal film location for period dramas—not to mention a popular destination for tourists to the Cotswolds—and now that Caitlyn had a chance to wander around the Manor, she was beginning to see why.

She was also beginning to wonder how the Fitzroy family had ever learned their way around the place. Just as she was about to give up and look for a member of the staff to ask directions, she found herself in a quieter wing of the house and, a moment later, wandered into the beautiful attached Victorian conservatory. It was a light, bright, airy space with panelled French windows and slanted glass ceilings, furnished with comfortable wicker sofas overflowing with floral cushions, as well as potted ferns, miniature orange trees, and climbing bougainvillea.

The sound of female giggles led Caitlyn to the far side of the conservatory where the glazed double doors were thrown open to let in the warmth of the June evening. She found Pomona curled up in a wicker chaise longue next to the doors, her head tilted flirtatiously as she laughed and talked with a young man standing in the open doorway.

Caitlyn smiled inwardly: so much for being worried about Pomona's state of mind. It looked like her cousin was fully recovered and back to her favourite hobby: flirting with any handsome male in the vicinity! She looked curiously at the young man talking to her cousin. He was dressed in faded jeans tucked into Wellington boots, and an old cotton shirt rolled up at the sleeves to show muscular forearms. He had the kind of striking good looks, coupled with jet black hair and bright blue eyes, which hinted at a Celtic ancestry, and this was confirmed when Caitlyn heard the Irish lilt in his voice.

"Caitlyn!" Pomona looked up in delight. "I thought you weren't gonna get over here today. Have you met Matt? He's one of the gardeners here at the estate."

"Hi..." Matt grinned and held up soil-stained hands. "Excuse me for not shaking. So you must be Pomona's cousin. I've been hearing a lot about you," he said with a knowing smile.

"I hope you don't believe everything you hear,"

said Caitlyn, laughing.

"Well, I must have got something wrong because I thought you lived in L.A. like Pomona here... but I don't hear much of an American accent," said Matt, cocking his head to one side.

"My... um... my mother was American, but we never lived in the States much. We travelled a lot," Caitlyn explained.

"It wasn't just that—it's 'cos Caitlyn had a British nanny who brought her up and taught her to talk funny," said Pomona with a wink to Matt. "I was always terrified whenever I visited them 'cos Nanny Rosemary would be like..." She put a hand on her waist and adopted an exaggerated British accent. *"...'Miss Pomona, I expect young ladies to enunciate their words properly. Please make sure you say "want to" instead of "wanna". The latter shows a deplorable carelessness and laziness in pronunciation.'"* She giggled.

"I'd hate to think what she'd say about my Irish lingo, then," said Matt with a chuckle. He looked back at Caitlyn. "So how come you travelled so much?"

"My mother was a singer, so we were often on tour or going to music festivals and things. Also, she was a real gypsy at heart. She had itchy feet and didn't like staying in one place."

"Aunt Barbara used to say it helped her write her songs better if she kept moving to new places," added Pomona. She glanced at her cousin. "But it

15

did mean that poor Caitlyn never got the chance to make friends much or feel like she belonged anywhere."

"Barbara? Oh, of course, Barbara Le Fey!" Matt snapped his fingers. "I should have made the connection with your last name. I've got a couple of her albums. Good stuff." He paused, then added, "Sorry to hear about her recent death."

"Thanks," Caitlyn said awkwardly. She was still uncomfortable that she didn't feel more grief at the loss of her adoptive mother. She and Barbara had never been close and when it was revealed to her, after the funeral, that she was adopted, it had almost been a relief. Still, she couldn't help feeling guilty—it had felt slightly like a betrayal to come to England so quickly after the funeral and search for her real family. And even now, although she had traced her roots to Tillyhenge, she felt uncertain about staying on...

"You're staying with that old witch in the village chocolate shop, aren't you?" Matt said. He laughed as he saw Caitlyn's expression. "Don't worry—I know most of the village is terrified of the Widow Mags but I'm not one of them. Hey, I'm Irish; we grow up with bedtime stories of monsters and faerie-folk. Besides, Mags has been good to me—she gave me a dock leaf salve that was grand. Cleared up my nettle rash in no time. Worked better than anything I bought at the chemist's." He winked. "Maybe she is a witch after all."

If only you knew, thought Caitlyn with a silent laugh. Aloud, she said, "Yes, I'm staying at *Bewitched by Chocolate*. There's a spare room above the shop."

"That's not a room," said Pomona. "You should see my bedroom here—now *that's* a room! I've stayed in some pretty fancy Hollywood mansions but this is something else. I really lucked out when James invited me to stay here to recover! I feel kinda bad that you have to sleep in that attic cupboard and I'm staying here in all this luxury."

"It's not that terrible," said Caitlyn, laughing. "Okay, so it's a bit small and a bit basic... but the chocolate more than makes up for it!"

Matt chuckled. "Yeah, I've had some of the Widow Mags's chocolates. Everyone says they must be enchanted by dark magic to taste so good." He smacked his lips. "Well, I say—if that's the truth, hex me all you want!"

"So what's your secret?" asked Pomona, tossing back her honey blonde hair and giving him a coy smile. "How d'you eat chocolates and, like, stay in such good shape?" She eyed Matt's biceps admiringly. "You must go to the gym to work out a lot, huh?"

Matt flexed his arms and grinned at her. "Nope, these muscles are a hundred percent natural. Just pure flowerbed-digging and wheelbarrow-pushing. No artificial weights or punchbags."

Pomona giggled. "I never realised gardening

could be so... healthy. Maybe I should get more into it."

"Well, now, I'd be delighted to show you around," said Matt, raising a suggestive eyebrow. "Especially the walled garden. You haven't seen anything until you've seen my herbaceous borders..."

How the man managed to make herbaceous borders sound sexy was a mystery. His flirting was outrageous and should never have been allowed in a member of the staff, but even Caitlyn couldn't help responding to the twinkle in his blue eyes. Matt had charm in bucketloads and he knew how to use it. Caitlyn wondered if Pomona might have met her match at last.

"O'Brien! What are ye doing there?" came an irate voice from outside the conservatory. "His Lordship is paying ye to tend his garden, not entertain his guests!"

Caitlyn turned to see an old man in green overalls standing behind the rosebushes and glowering at Matt from beneath bushy eyebrows. It was Old Palmer, the Head Gardener.

"Feck! Duty calls," said Matt with a careless smile. He swept them an exaggerated bow, which had Pomona giggling again, then turned and strolled off, whistling jauntily.

"Omigod—he's so hot! That Lady Chatterley was on to something. I think I'm in love..." Pomona sighed dreamily.

Caitlyn looked at her askance. "I thought you

were in love last week?"

"Yeah, well, that was before I found out that my date was a lizard. Like, literally." Pomona shot her a dark look. Then she grinned and stretched out on the chaise longue. "Anyway, plenty more fish in the sea, as they say. In fact, plenty more fish right here in Huntingdon Manor! Who'd have thought there'd be, like, so many hunks in this little corner of England? Here's this sexy-as-sin Irish gardener... and of course, there's your handsome British lord—"

"He's not my lord," said Caitlyn quickly.

"Well, he's not gonna be if you keep looking like that!" said Pomona, screwing up her face. "Omigod, Caitlyn, what's with the dress? It's, like, the ugliest thing I've ever seen!"

"It's not mine—it's one of the maid's uniforms. I got drenched walking over here so I had to borrow this while they're drying my clothes." Caitlyn looked out through the conservatory windows and sighed. "Anyway, it wouldn't make much difference. I'm not you, Pomie," she said, looking back at her cousin with wistful envy.

With her golden tan and voluptuous figure, not to mention her sparkling brown eyes and generous mouth, Pomona was striking in anyone's book. But it was really her confidence that set her apart. Whereas Caitlyn agonized over her hips and thighs, Pomona flaunted hers in tightfitting skirts and jeans that drew every male eye in the room. No one could look away when Pomona wriggled her bottom and the last thing you thought about was its size.

"That's crap!" said Pomona. "Honey, you could look so gorgeous if you just made a bit of effort. I mean—look at your hair! There are women who would kill to get red hair like that. And your eyes.... You've got, like, the perfect hazel eyes. You could make them look green or gold or brown, depending on the eye-shadow and what you're wearing... C'mon! Lemme do a makeover! You'll look so fantastic—"

Caitlyn shook her head and laughed. This was a repeat of the conversation they had practically every time Pomona saw her. Her cousin had been begging her for years to let her transform her look and Caitlyn had always resisted. For one thing, she didn't really believe it could be done, and for another... well, to be honest, Caitlyn was scared. If she *did* let Pomona transform her, she would have to put herself out there, deal with getting attention, face people looking at her and judging her. It seemed safer just to stay drab and unremarkable, to remain a wallflower in the shadows.

Although... for a fleeting moment, Caitlyn wondered wistfully what it would be like to appear glamorous and beautiful for once, in front of James Fitzroy, instead of the frumpy mess she always seemed to be in. Then she pushed the thought away, chiding herself for the silly fantasy. James must be surrounded by gorgeous society girls all the time—how did she think that she could ever compete?

As if reading her mind, Pomona grinned and said, "You could totally wow James, you know. I mean, the guy's already falling for you big time— you could knock his socks off."

Caitlyn blushed furiously. "There's nothing between James and me."

Pomona made a rude noise. "Yeah right. Have you seen the way he looks at you? Seriously, the guy finds you attractive even when you walk around looking like a sack of mouldy potatoes. He's the kind of man who can see—" Pomona lowered her voice dramatically, "—'inner beauty'. Those men practically don't exist! D'you know how lucky you are? He's like... like an endangered species! But you gotta help the poor guy out. Let him see some of your 'outer beauty' too."

Caitlyn sighed and shook her head again. "Pomie, it's not that simple. I mean... I'm not even sure if I'm staying in Tillyhenge."

Her cousin's mouth dropped open. "What? You're not seriously thinking of leaving?"

Caitlyn shrugged. "I don't know... I keep thinking that I can still... you know, close this chapter in my life, turn the page and move on. Go back to London, maybe even go back to the States. Like... forget it ever happened."

Pomona gave her a glassy stare. "You think you can really forget everything that's happened? You've gotta be kidding me! You've seen magic, Caitlyn! You've *used* it! That's not something you just forget—like that." She snapped her fingers.

"Everyone has weird things happen to them sometimes, right?" said Caitlyn desperately. "Strange coincidences, unexplained phenomena... They just shrug it off and say it's a mystery and move on. Get back to their lives."

"Aww, for pity's sake!" said Pomona in exasperation. "There's no way you can go back to the way it was before. I mean, *come on*! You're a witch! You can, like, do awesome stuff with magic. Why would you wanna turn your back on that? Jeez, if I discovered I had witch blood in my veins, I'd be all over a spell so fast, you wouldn't have time to say 'cauldron'!"

Caitlyn laughed in spite of herself. That was another thing she envied about Pomona: her cousin's easy faith and acceptance of the supernatural. It helped, of course, that Pomona had always been obsessed with the occult and had spent a lot of her spare time dabbling in everything from tarot cards to crystal healing. When she had arrived in Tillyhenge and discovered that witchcraft and magic *did* exist, Pomona had barely batted an eyelid. In fact, she had jumped in and embraced the new reality with great glee. Pomona was *delighted* that witches and magic spells were real—it was what she had been telling everybody all along!

Still, Caitlyn had to admit that once she had got

over her own disbelief and scepticism, Pomona was right. There *was* something wonderful, incredible, amazing about discovering that you were a witch, that you could control magic, that witchcraft didn't just exist in fairy tales and movies...

"And you're not just any old witch," Pomona continued eagerly. "I mean, it would be pretty awesome already if you could cast spells and create potions... but you can do this amazing thing with *chocolate*. Like, tap into all that latent magic in *cacao*, all the stuff that the ancient Aztecs and Mayans knew... Seriously, how cool is it to have that as your heritage?" She sighed ecstatically. "Magic and *chocolate*! Omigod, how can you say no to that?"

"Okay, okay, you've made your point," said Caitlyn with a chuckle. "I'm not saying it would be *easy* to turn my back on it all. I just... I don't know... Everything's been a bit overwhelming since the funeral and finding out I'm adopted... and then arriving in Tillyhenge... and this whole 'witch' thing..." She trailed off helplessly.

"Hey..." said Pomona softly, her brown eyes turning serious. She reached out and squeezed Caitlyn's hand. "I understand. It must have been a horrible shock for you, especially the adoption thing."

"Finding out that my whole life was a lie, you mean."

"Not all of it!" Pomona protested. "I mean, we

23

might not be related by blood, but you'll always be my cousin. My family."

Caitlyn smiled, feeling a rush of love for the other girl. Though they hadn't lived in the same city, Pomona had often come out during her school vacations and joined Barbara Le Fey's travelling entourage, so the two girls had spent a lot of time together growing up. Pomona was more than just her cousin—she was her best friend.

"Thanks, Pomie. You know I feel the same about you," she said, squeezing the other girl's hand in return.

"As long as you remember that when you find your real family," Pomona said jokingly.

"Actually, speaking of that..." Caitlyn hesitated.

Pomona pounced on her. "What? Have you found something new?"

CHAPTER THREE

Caitlyn reached beneath the collar of her dress and pulled out a runestone attached to a ribbon. She had worn it around her neck ever since she could remember—in fact, ever since she had been found as a baby.

She held the runestone up to Pomona. "You know I showed this to Bertha and the Widow Mags—"

"Yeah, I remember—you said they both freaked out, and then refused to talk about it."

"Yes, but I got the impression that Bertha would have said more, if her mother hadn't been there."

"Well, the Widow Mags can be pretty scary, you know. I mean, I wouldn't even blink if she told me not to."

Caitlyn gave her cousin a playful shove. "Don't

give me that! You're not scared of her—I saw the way you stood up to her when you wanted to give the chocolate shop a makeover."

"Yeah, but you didn't see my knees shaking!" said Pomona, grinning. "I kept waiting for her to zap me and turn me into a toad."

Caitlyn laughed. "Actually, I think you won her over with your sass. It's probably refreshing to have someone talk back to her for once."

"So what's this got to do with your real family?"

"Well, the night after we found you—when you were still in the hospital—I was back at the chocolate shop and I got Bertha alone for a moment, so I asked her about it again." Caitlyn paused significantly. "And she showed me a runestone around her own neck, just like mine!"

"Holy cow!" Pomona sat up. "Do you mean... Bertha and the Widow Mags are—"

"I don't know. We got interrupted. The Widow Mags came out and basically told Bertha to keep her mouth shut. She said: 'There are things that should stay in the past'."

"What did she mean by that?"

Caitlyn heaved a sigh of frustration. "I don't know! That's all she would say. And then Bertha clammed up after that."

"So ask her again!"

"I haven't really had a chance to speak to her without the Widow Mags being around."

"I know!" said Pomona. "Go to *Herbal*

Enchantments—Bertha's store—and talk to her there. Then the Widow Mags wouldn't know about it."

"Don't count on it," said Caitlyn darkly. "She always seems to know everything." Then she brightened. "But that's a good idea, Pomie. I'll try to do that."

"Imagine... the Widow Mags could be your grandmother! She'd be the right age for it. And Bertha could be—" Pomona gasped. "Do you think she could be your mother?"

Slowly, Caitlyn shook her head. "No, I don't think so. I can't really explain it but I feel like... well, if she was my mother, I'd know. I'd feel it—in here." She pressed her hand to her heart. "And anyway, wouldn't she say something if she was? I can't believe that she would just keep quiet about it..."

"Okay, well, maybe she could be your aunt! That would make Evie your cousin. Your sweet English cousin," Pomona added, grinning. She leaned back and fluffed her hair. "As opposed to your sexy American cousin."

Caitlyn laughed. "You're one of a kind, Pomona, whatever country you're from."

A sound from the doorway leading back into the house made them both look up. A minute later, something scampered into the conservatory: a fluffy black kitten. He was followed by an enormous English mastiff the size of a small pony, who lumbered in after the kitten, his baggy wrinkled face pulled back in a happy doggie grin. They seemed to be playing a game of hide 'n' seek, although mostly it was just the kitten hiding and the mastiff looking very confused.

"Hello, you!" said Caitlyn in delight, reaching down to scoop up the kitten as he scampered past. He looked up at her with big yellow eyes and let out a loud "*Meew!*"

Caitlyn smiled. The first time she had seen this kitten, he had been a terrified little thing fighting for his life in a quarry pond and she had rescued him just in time from drowning. Now he was a cheeky scamp, with a little round tummy and glossy black fur that stood out from his body in spiky tufts.

"*Meew!*" he said again, starting to squirm in her grasp, and Caitlyn chuckled. "All right, all right... Here you go..." She put him down on the floor again and the kitten instantly scampered off in search of his big friend.

"They're so cute together," said Pomona, smiling as she watched them. "I swear, the first time I saw that dog, I nearly freaked out. I thought he was gonna squash the kitten. But he's so gentle..."

"Yeah, he's a gentle giant. Hello, Bran... Aren't you a gorgeous boy...?" Caitlyn cooed as the mastiff came up to them and thrust his jowly face into her lap. He stood and drooled on her as she patted him.

"Er... yeah, gorgeous except for the slobber," said Pomona, edging away. She glanced up through the conservatory windows and a gleam came into her eyes. "Ooh! Guess who's coming this way? Hmm... I think I need to pop back to my room to get something..."

"Wha—?" Caitlyn turned and looked out of the conservatory window, then her eyes widened in alarm. "No, wait, Pomie, don't go—"

Too late. Pomona was already hurrying out of the conservatory and, a moment later, James Fitzroy stepped in through the open double doors from the garden.

"Caitlyn... there you are! I was wondering where you'd got to." He smiled as he came over to join her.

"Er, hi..." Caitlyn shifted uncomfortably and started to stand up, then realised that not only was she wearing a hideous dress which was stretched across her hips, showing every bulge of her thighs, but she was now also covered in dog drool.

Great, thought Caitlyn with a silent groan. So much for meeting James looking beautiful and glamorous...! She looked around frantically, grabbed a cushion at random and held it on her lap, hoping that it would hide both fat and slobber.

"Are you all right?" asked James, looking at her slightly quizzically.

"Er... yes, fine, fine! Just enjoying your conservatory furniture... Lov-ely cushions!" Caitlyn said brightly, manically stroking the one on her lap like a Bond villain.

"Thank you." James looked at her uncertainly. He sat down in a wicker armchair opposite her.

"Where's Pomona? I thought she was here in the conservatory?"

"She's gone up to her room to get something," mumbled Caitlyn, adding silently that she was going to kill her cousin the next time she saw her.

There was an awkward silence and Caitlyn squirmed, trying to think of something to say. Then, to her relief, the black kitten bounded past.

"Ah, here you are, you little monkey!" James said with a laugh. He reached down and scooped up the baby cat, lifting him up to face level. The kitten raised a paw and batted playfully at James's nose. "*Meew!*"

James looked at Caitlyn over the top of the furry head, his grey eyes laughing. "You know, all the staff are besotted with him—and half the tourists too. I keep having to stop little old ladies trying to smuggle him home in their handbags."

"What are you going to call him?" asked Caitlyn.

"Well... I thought I'd let you decide," said James with a smile as he put the kitten back down. "After all, we did rescue him together so I suppose you could say that he is 'our' cat."

Caitlyn dropped her eyes and busied herself patting the kitten, hoping that he wouldn't see the blush heating her cheeks. Somehow the way he said that made it all sound so intimate.

She cleared her throat. "I... I haven't really got any ideas."

"There's no hurry. Wait until inspiration strikes

you." James chuckled. "At the moment, he seems to be getting along fine either being called: 'Aren't you adorable?' by the women staff or 'Oi! Ye bloody cat!' by Old Palmer, when he catches him digging in the gardens."

Caitlyn laughed and was about to reply when there was a commotion in the hallway outside and, the next moment, a middle-aged woman came barging into the conservatory, followed by a harassed-looking maid.

"Mrs Winifred Harris, sir," said the maid. "She insisted on seeing you."

"He knows who I am!" snapped the woman.

She looked vaguely familiar and Caitlyn realised that she had seen Winifred Harris once or twice around the village, gossiping with other residents and bossily directing tourists. She was in her late fifties and had stiff permed hair and a stolid, respectable face—the kind of woman you expected to be presiding over church committees and organising charity fundraisers.

She strode towards James now, brandishing a folder on which Caitlyn could see a label with the words "*Fitzroy Summer Garden Party*" in carefully written letters.

"Lord Fitzroy! This is an absolute outrage!" she cried. "I knew it had to be a mistake so I came to see you immediately."

James rose politely. "Mrs Harris—is something the matter?"

"Yes!" The woman faced James and pulled herself up to her full height. "I have just been going over the final menu for the Garden Party and the list of items that are going to be served... and I noticed that there is a new section. *Chocolates!*" She nearly spat out the word. "Chocolates from the Widow Mags's shop in the village!"

"Is there a problem with that?" asked James, looking puzzled.

Mrs Harris gave him a lofty look. "You may not realise it, Lord Fitzroy, but that woman has a... a reputation."

"You're not referring to the silly nonsense about her being a witch, I hope?"

"It's not nonsense!" said Mrs Harris indignantly. "She *is* a witch! Everyone knows it. She has even cursed several of the ladies in the village—just ask Angela Skinner! They suffered terribly just because they dared to go into that chocolate shop of hers. The Widow Mags put a hex on them and gave them warts!"

James sighed. "Mrs Harris, the police investigated that incident and found no evidence of wrongdoing on the Widow Mags's part. In fact, from what I heard, Miss Skinner mistook a blob of chocolate on her nose for a... er... unusual skin growth."

"What about what happened with the cup of hot chocolate?" Mrs Harris demanded. "There was no earthly explanation for that! It just erupted in

Angela's face!"

James glanced at Caitlyn, who squirmed in her seat. She knew the truth about that hot chocolate incident and she had already been forced to lie to James once—she didn't want it all raked up again.

"I am not sure what happened there but, again, the police did not feel the need to investigate further," said James patiently. "I appreciate your concerns, Mrs Harris, but I assure you that they are unfounded. The Widow Mags is a longstanding member of the village and a skilled chocolatier. I think it would be wonderful to have her creations at the Garden Party for everyone to sample. Her chocolates are delicious, probably the best I've ever tasted—"

"Yes, and don't you wonder why?" demanded Mrs Harris. "They're bewitched, that's what they are! Bewitched by dark magic! That's why they taste so good. And they make you feel... all manner of things. It's downright sinful!"

James burst out laughing. "Mrs Harris, I think they are simply very good chocolates. There is no sinister magic in that."

"She has bewitched you too!" declared Mrs Harris. "That's right. She's got to you, Lord Fitzroy. Otherwise, you'd never be standing there, condoning such evil decadence. Ohhh, your father is probably turning in his grave! He would never have allowed the Widow Mags's chocolates to be served at the Garden Party when he was head of

Huntingdon Manor!"

James's grey eyes turned cold. "Perhaps you are right, Mrs Harris. But *I* am the head of Huntingdon Manor now and I have decided to include the chocolates on the menu. It's high time that this ridiculous prejudice against the Widow Mags is put to an end. Her chocolates are of exemplary quality and I have no doubt that they would be greatly enjoyed by the villagers, if everyone could just overlook such irrational fears and malicious hearsay. I am sorry if that offends your sensibilities but I am not prepared to discuss this further."

Caitlyn looked at James in silent awe. His voice was still calm and infallibly polite, but there was no mistaking the steel in his tone or the quiet authority in his manner.

Mrs Harris flushed angrily but she seemed to realise that she had gone too far. "It is your event, of course, Lord Fitzroy," she said tightly. "But don't say I didn't warn you! Letting a witch and her wicked chocolates into the Garden Party... you will regret it! Nothing but bad luck will come of that!"

Giving them all a last glare, she turned and stormed out of the room.

CHAPTER FOUR

Caitlyn walked slowly down the hallway towards Mrs Brixton's sitting room and paused outside. The door was shut but she could hear the muffled sound of raised voices coming from inside. She winced, wondering what she might be interrupting this time. After the unpleasant scene with Mrs Harris in the conservatory, the last thing she wanted to do was walk into another argument.

Then she noticed the pile of dry clothes neatly folded on top of the cabinet next to the door. She recognised them as hers. Delighted that she wouldn't have to see the housekeeper again, Caitlyn grabbed the clothes, changed quickly in the bathroom, and then let herself out of the rear entrance of the Manor.

James Fitzroy had offered to drive her back but

she had declined, deciding that she would enjoy the fresh air and exercise. Now she wondered if she should have taken him up on his offer. It wasn't raining but the sky was still grey and there were ominous clouds on the horizon. It was also getting dark. Normally the long summer days would have ensured that she'd have light until at least nine o'clock and have no trouble finding her way. Today, though, with the darkened skies and imminent rain, it felt like twilight was already falling.

Caitlyn set off at a brisk pace, hoping to make it back this time without getting wet. As she neared the top, Caitlyn glanced to her left where the forest flowed up the side of the hill and clung to its slopes, half covering it like a dark green blanket. Sitting on the crest of the hill, just at the edge of the forest, was an ancient stone circle. The misshapen boulders seemed almost to glow in the evening light, outlined against the darkness of the trees beyond. This was the Tillyhenge stone circle: the subject of countless myths and superstitions and—some said—the source of powerful magic.

A week ago, before she had arrived at Tillyhenge, Caitlyn would have scoffed at the legends surrounding this circle of sarsen boulders but now she was not so complacent. She had seen enough to know that witchcraft and magic did exist, and even what seemed like silly folk stories weren't to be taken lightly.

She looked thoughtfully at the stone circle as she

drew near. She hadn't paid it much attention earlier when she had passed it on her way to the Manor, too preoccupied with avoiding the rain, but now she looked at it again with the unease she always felt whenever she came here. There was something about the stones—some vibe—which could be felt, even if you didn't believe in magic or the paranormal. She had felt it that morning when she'd first seen them, even though she had still been sceptical of their associated myths and legends.

Then there had been that mysterious bonfire she'd seen from her bedroom window on her first night in Tillyhenge. Who had lit a bonfire here at the circle in the middle of the night? The villagers had denied any knowledge of it, although it was obvious that some of them were hiding something, whilst the police had shrugged it off as teenage arsonists. Maybe they were right... but somehow, Caitlyn didn't believe it.

She sighed to herself. Yet another mystery surrounding Tillyhenge. The village seemed to be full of them. She was about to turn away when she paused, her gaze sharpening as she realised that there was a figure on the other side of the circle—a young woman loitering around the tallest boulder.

Curious, Caitlyn went closer. A twig snapped underfoot, and the woman jumped and looked up. Their eyes met and Caitlyn stopped in surprise. It was Angela Skinner, a young woman who lived in the village. Caitlyn hesitated. She hadn't known Angela for long but she had seen enough to know that the other woman was a petty-minded, malicious bully. Still, Angela had suffered two very humiliating experiences recently and Caitlyn felt partly responsible.

Guilt made her offer the other woman a friendly smile as she called out, "Hi, Angela. It's a nice evening, isn't it? I'm so glad the rain stopped at last."

Angela stared at her for a moment, then pointedly turned her back and looked the other way, her nose in the air. Caitlyn flushed at the deliberate snub. She started to say something, then changed her mind. It wasn't worth it. Trying to put Angela out of her mind, she descended the other side of the hill, making her way down to the cottage nestled at the foot of the slope.

The rich aroma of chocolate hit her as she approached the rear of the cottage and Caitlyn could feel her mouth watering even before she stepped through the back door and into the kitchen. A riotous scene met her eyes: huge pots of melted chocolate being slowly stirred, dollops of creamy ganache being piped into crisp chocolate shells, trays of chocolate fudge brownies being taken out of ovens, and bowls of fluffy chocolate mousse being whipped into soft peaks... This would all have been perfectly normal at the back of any chocolate shop, except that here, the stirring ladles, hovering trays, and beating whisks were all moving by themselves. There was no human hand holding them. Caitlyn had seen it all before and yet she still felt like rubbing her eyes. No matter how many times she experienced it, she couldn't get over the thrill of seeing magic in action.

And in the centre of it all, directing everything with expert flicks of her gnarled hands, stood a hunched old woman. She had a face that had been written about a dozen times in children's books and fairy tales: dark arched eyebrows, piercing eyes, and a large, hooked nose … all that was missing was the black witch's hat and flying broomstick. But Caitlyn knew that the Widow Mags didn't need those clichéd embellishments. She was the real deal.

The old woman looked up as Caitlyn entered and growled, "About time, girl! Where have you been? I've been waiting for ages. I need someone to taste my chocolate fudge."

As she spoke, she waved a hand and a dark brown square lifted from a tray on the table and floated through the air towards Caitlyn, who took an involuntary step backwards. The square of fudge stopped and hovered in front of her mouth.

"Well, go on!" said the Widow Mags impatiently. "Tell me how it tastes!"

Caitlyn plucked the piece of fudge out of the air and popped it between her lips. She closed her eyes as a burst of rich chocolate flavour filled her mouth:

smooth, soft, creamy, and delicious, the fudge melted on her tongue and left a lingering taste of bittersweet chocolate and buttery caramel, as well as a hint of salty crunch.

She swallowed and opened her eyes. "That was *amazing*! What flavour is it? I've never tasted fudge like that."

"It's dark chocolate caramel with a hint of Celtic sea salt," said the Widow Mags, a pleased smile transforming her stern features. "It's one of the flavours I'm making for the Fitzroy Garden Party." She waved her hand again and two more pieces of fudge floated through the air towards Caitlyn. "Try these and tell me what you think."

Obediently, Caitlyn reached for the squares. The first was a heavenly blend of smooth milk chocolate and creamy peanut butter, the second a velvety chocolate fudge centre swirled through with sumptuous vanilla.

"They're both absolutely divine!" said Caitlyn, licking her fingers and eyeing the trays greedily, wondering if she could have another piece. There seemed to be rows upon rows of fudge spread out across the wooden table in the centre of the kitchen. "Wow... how many different kinds did you make?"

The Widow Mags waved a hand and said casually, "Oh, well, when Lord Fitzroy asked me to provide some things for the Garden Party, I thought I'd rustle up a few different flavours. There's traditional toffee, of course, and the chocolate caramel, Belgian chocolate and vanilla, and peanut butter swirl, which you tasted..." She led the way to the shop area at the front of the cottage and pointed to another tray on the counter, filled with squares of dark brown fudge drizzled with white chocolate and topped with juicy red fruit. "...And I'm also trying a dark chocolate laced with Morello cherries and brandy. Of course, the centerpiece is going to be the triple-layered chocolate fudge cake. That has to be made fresh the day before the party but it won't take me long."

She was trying to sound like she didn't really care but Caitlyn could see that beneath the false nonchalance, the Widow Mags was beaming with pride. The old woman would probably never admit it but she was delighted to have been asked to provide sweet treats for the Garden Party menu. Caitlyn felt a flash of gratitude towards James for having the kindness and generosity to include an old woman so many others had ignored and ostracised.

Still, the Widow Mags hadn't made things easy for herself either, Caitlyn admitted ruefully. The old witch was as prickly as a hedgehog, hiding her warm wisdom and genuine kindness beneath a gruff manner and cranky demeanour. And with her unfortunate dowager's hump and fierce appearance, it was no wonder that the villagers were terrified of her and thought her to be an evil old hag.

As if echoing her thoughts, there came the sound

of a gasp from the direction of the street. Caitlyn turned and caught sight of a small face pressed against the shop window, peering into the store. It was a little girl of about six years old, with a snub nose and short brown pigtails. She was staring at the Widow Mags through the glass, her mouth open in a wide O and her eyes terrified.

Caitlyn started towards the open shop door, a reassuring smile on her face, but before she had taken a few steps, the face was gone. The little girl had run away.

"What was that?" asked the Widow Mags.

Caitlyn threw a last look at the empty window pane. "Nothing." She turned back to the Widow Mags and gave her a hopeful smile. "So... are there any more fudge flavours you'd like me to taste?"

***

Caitlyn climbed into bed and groaned slightly, rubbing her stomach. She hated to admit it but she had probably eaten way too much fudge. She shuddered to think how many calories she had consumed this afternoon. She could practically feel her thighs growing thicker as she lay in bed.

The absurdity of that image made her giggle and she turned over, snuggling deeper into the pillow. She wouldn't eat any chocolates tomorrow, she promised herself. *Absolutely not. Not even one mouthful.* Her eyelids drooped and she felt herself drifting into sleep…

THUMP! THUMP! THUMP! THUMP!

Caitlyn sat bolt upright in bed, her heart pounding. Somebody was banging on the front door downstairs, she realised. She jumped out of bed, still barefoot and in her sleep T-shirt, and hurried into the shop below. The Widow Mags was already opening the front door to a grey-haired man in a sombre suit, accompanied by a uniformed constable.

"Inspector Walsh!" Caitlyn said in surprise, recognising the CID detective.

"I hope you have a good reason for barging in here like this, at this hour of the night," growled the Widow Mags.

"We do, ma'am," said the inspector, his face grim. "There's been a murder at Huntingdon Manor."

CHAPTER FIVE

Caitlyn gasped. "A murder? Who's been killed? Pomona—is she okay? What about James—I mean, Lord Fitzroy?"

"They are both fine," the inspector assured her. "The victim is Mrs Brixton, the housekeeper."

"The housekeeper?" said the Widow Mags. "Who would want to murder her?"

"That's what we're trying to find out, ma'am," said the inspector. He looked speculatively at Caitlyn. "I'd like to ask you a few questions please, Miss Le Fey."

"Uh... sure," said Caitlyn, surprised at his tone.

"I understand that you were at Huntingdon Manor this afternoon?"

Caitlyn nodded. "I walked over to see my cousin, Pomona, who went to stay there after she was discharged from the hospital."

"And did you see Mrs Brixton?"

"Yes, I got drenched in the downpour on the way there. Mrs Brixton got me some towels and a temporary dress to wear while she dried my clothes."

"And how long did you stay at the Manor?"

Caitlyn shrugged. "Probably around an hour and a half? Maybe two hours? I remember arriving around five-thirty and I'm not sure when I left. I think it might have been around seven-thirty."

"What were you doing during the time you were at the Manor?"

Caitlyn looked at him curiously, wondering how this was relevant to the murder. "Well, after I dried off and changed, I went to find my cousin. She was in the conservatory... and then James—Lord Fitzroy—came to join us. I mean, me. My cousin had gone up to her room. We... um... chatted for a bit. Then I left soon after."

"Did you see anyone else during your time at the Manor?"

"I saw some of the staff... and a group of tourists. Oh, and Winifred Harris from the village. She arrived to speak to Lord Fitzroy just before I left."

"What about?"

Caitlyn squirmed, conscious of the Widow Mags listening. "Um... just about arrangements for the Garden Party."

"And which members of the staff did you see,

aside from Mrs Brixton?"

"Well, there was one of the gardeners—Matt O'Brien—and Old Palmer, the Head Gardener. And there was a maid who showed Mrs Harris in... Two maids, actually," said Caitlyn, remembering the conversation she had overheard outside Mrs Brixton's sitting room.

"Yes?" said Inspector Walsh sharply, his eyes suddenly alert.

Caitlyn shifted uncomfortably. She didn't enjoy feeling like a snitch but she couldn't really refuse to answer the inspector either. "When I went to give Mrs Brixton my wet clothes, I overheard her having an argument with Amelia, one of the maids, in her sitting room."

"Did you hear what the argument was about?"

"Er... it sounded like Mrs Brixton had caught Amelia stealing something and she was... she was asking for money to keep quiet about it."

Inspector Walsh raised his eyebrows. "Are you telling me that Mrs Brixton was trying to blackmail the maid?"

Caitlyn shifted even more uncomfortably. "Yes. That's what it sounded like."

"And what did the maid try to steal?"

"I don't know. I didn't hear. Mrs Brixton did mention silver but I don't know if that was what Amelia tried to take."

"What do you mean, you don't know? Why would Mrs Brixton mention silver—"

"She was saying that as an example. Amelia started saying that she wasn't really stealing for herself and Mrs Brixton said: 'all thieves say that when they try to make off with the silver'—or something like that."

"I see." Inspector Walsh was silent for a moment, then asked, "And did you see Mrs Brixton again after that?"

"N-no... I went back to the old servants' quarters to get my clothes before I left, but I didn't see her. I found my clothes already dry so I just changed and let myself out."

"And what did you do after leaving the Manor?"

"I came back here," said Caitlyn, looking at him with some surprise.

"What time did you get back?"

"Um... I don't know... it takes about twenty minutes to walk the shortcut over the hill... I guess it must have been around eight o'clock?"

"It was just gone eight," the Widow Mags spoke up. "I know because I was baking and I had the timer set for the next batch to go in the oven."

"And I assume you would be willing to stand up and swear that in a court of law?" asked the inspector.

The Widow Mags's eyebrows drew together. "Of course I would. But why would I need to do that? You're not suggesting that you suspect *Caitlyn* of murdering Mrs Brixton?"

The inspector's face was impassive. "The forensic

pathologist has done a preliminary examination and—together with the times the victim was last seen by other witnesses and the discovery of her body—it appears that Mrs Brixton was killed sometime between a quarter past seven and eight o'clock." He looked at Caitlyn. "One of the garden boys reports that he saw you leaving via the back door of the Manor in a hurried manner."

Caitlyn frowned. "Well, of course I was hurrying! I was worried it might rain again. I wanted to get back here quickly. Also, it was getting late and the light was fading."

"The sun doesn't set until nine-thirty at this time of the year."

"Yes, but it had been raining all day and the skies were grey already, so it was getting pretty dark."

"Nevertheless, you cannot deny that you were at the scene of the crime during the time the murder took place."

"Well, I—" Caitlyn broke off and stared at the inspector. She felt an uneasy chill at his accusatory tone. "This is crazy! Are you really saying you think I murdered Mrs Brixton?"

"You do not seem to have an alibi for the time of the murder. Lord Fitzroy says he said goodbye to you at around seven-twenty, when you went to fetch your clothes from Mrs Brixton. The Widow Mags here can vouch for you being back at the chocolate shop by eight o'clock. But that still leaves over thirty minutes unaccounted for." He leaned forwards. "And for your information, one can do the walk over the hill, from Huntingdon Manor to this cottage, in about fifteen minutes, if you jog. I checked. So in theory, you could have murdered Mrs Brixton then set off from the Manor and been back here by eight. You had ample time to do it and no one saw you during that time."

"No, wait..." Caitlyn brightened. "Someone did see me. I met Angela Skinner up by the stone circle and said hello to her. That must have been just around seven-forty-five... She can testify that I was at the top of the hill by then."

The inspector said nothing but Caitlyn thought that his expression softened slightly.

"Well, that would certainly change things. I shall speak to Miss Skinner at the first opportunity to confirm your alibi," he said. "In the meantime, I'd like to ask you to accompany me back to the Manor and take a look at the crime scene, see if there is anything you notice. You were one of the last people to see Mrs Brixton alive."

Caitlyn swallowed. "Yes, sure. Just give me a minute to get dressed and put some shoes on."

Twenty minutes later, she found herself being escorted into the housekeeper's sitting room. She braced herself slightly as she entered, even though she knew that the body would have already been removed.

Inspector Walsh gestured around the room.

"Please take a look around, Miss Le Fey, and tell me if it looks any different to when you were here earlier this afternoon."

Caitlyn scanned the room. "No... Everything looks pretty much the same, I think... Oh, there was a big jug on the mantelpiece over there. One of those vintage water jugs, in blue and white china. It's gone."

"Yes," said Inspector Walsh. "It was used as the murder weapon."

"Oh." Caitlyn drew back slightly at the implication. "You mean... that was used to kill—?"

The inspector nodded. "The murderer smashed it against the back of Mrs Brixton's head. She was probably killed instantly."

"The back of her head?" Caitlyn mused. "That means Mrs Brixton must have turned her back on the murderer... which means that she probably trusted him or her."

"Very good," said the inspector with reluctant admiration. "You're a smart girl. Yes, there are no signs of forced entry either so we believe that Mrs Brixton knew and trusted her killer. She was taken by surprise."

"Can't you check the water jug for fingerprints—?"

"The SOCO team have been working on the crime scene and they will certainly be checking for prints. However, since the jug smashed into several small pieces, it might be hard to lift a clear print. In particular, the handle is missing and that is probably where the murderer gripped the jug. He or she must have taken it with them." He gestured around the room again. "Anything else?"

Caitlyn looked around once more, then her gaze sharpened. "There." She pointed. "There was a bunch of keys on the desk."

"A bunch of keys?"

"Yes, you know, one of those big, old-fashioned rings, with lots of keys on it. Mrs Brixton always carried it around. She was holding it when I first saw her this afternoon and later, when I came here to give her my wet clothes, I noticed them on the desk. But perhaps they were found on her?"

The inspector shook his head. "No, there were no keys found on her person."

"So that means the murderer took them, doesn't it?" asked Caitlyn excitedly.

Inspector Walsh made a non-committal noise. "I will need to check with Lord Fitzroy and see what the keys were for—I assume there is a duplicate set." He put a hand under Caitlyn's elbow. "Thank you for that, Miss Le Fey. You have been very helpful. Now, if you'll come with me, we will rejoin Lord Fitzroy and your cousin in the library."

They walked silently back through the house until they reached the library. As soon as Caitlyn stepped in, she found herself enveloped in a hug.

"Caitlyn!" Pomona squeezed her tight. "Omigod, I thought they'd thrown you in jail! Don't say anything to the police! I'm gonna get on the phone to Mom's attorney back in Hollywood—he's, like, the best in the business; they don't call him 'Rottweiler Randy' for nothing! I'll get some of my paparazzi contacts on it too. Hah, see if the police dare harass you once the media are involved! I've been trying to share it on social media but the internet here is beyond crappy! James says there's, like, a black spot over Tillyhenge or something, but, like, seriously? Anyway, don't worry, once I get on Facebook, I'll share it everywhere so that everyone knows about your wrongful arrest—"

Pomona paused to draw breath at last and Caitlyn quickly cut in, "I'm fine, Pomie. Calm down. The police have just been asking me some questions, that's all."

Inspector Walsh cleared his throat. "There is no question of arresting Miss Le Fey... yet."

Pomona glared at him. "Well, it's a joke that you'd even have her as a suspect! I mean, why would she wanna kill Mrs Brixton? She hardly even knew her!"

"Miss Le Fey is one of the last people to see the victim alive and she was also seen in the vicinity at the time of the murder. We are simply doing our job. We have to check everyone's alibi—that's just the way it is." Inspector Walsh turned to Caitlyn. "Once we speak to Angela Skinner and verify your whereabouts with her, I imagine your alibi will have some substance. In the meantime, however, I would advise you to remain in the area and to let the police know if you are thinking of leaving Tillyhenge." His voice was pleasant but there was a warning in his tone.

Caitlyn nodded, then watched numbly as the inspector turned to James and began asking him about the ring of keys. By the time the police finally left, she was struggling to stay on her feet as a wave of tiredness hit her. The adrenalin and excitement from the unexpected news of the murder had faded, leaving her drained and exhausted.

"It's very late," said James, looking at her in concern. "I'd be happy to drop you back at the chocolate shop but would you like to stay here for the night?"

"Yeah, stay!" urged Pomona.

"Thanks," said Caitlyn gratefully, trying to hide a yawn behind her hand. "That sounds great."

A few minutes later, after bidding James and Pomona goodnight, she was shown to one of the guest bedrooms: an elegant suite decorated in muted shades of cream and gold, with an enormous oak bed overflowing with cushions and pillows, and an en-suite bathroom with a vintage clawfoot bath. After the events of the last few hours, it all felt slightly surreal—as if she had suddenly checked into a luxury country hotel for the night.

Caitlyn cleaned her teeth, then climbed wearily into the huge bed. It was far more luxurious than the bed she had climbed into at the chocolate shop a couple of hours ago, and yet—with her mind still buzzing—it was a long time before she finally drifted off to sleep.

CHAPTER SIX

When she opened her eyes the next morning, Caitlyn had to struggle for a moment to remember where she was. She turned her head on the soft feather pillow and felt the satiny sheets beneath her fingers as she looked around in confusion. Sunlight was streaming in through the gaps in the curtains at the huge Jacobean-style bay windows, highlighting the cream and gold décor of the room and reflecting off the edge of the three-panelled mirror on the antique dressing table.

Caitlyn sat up and sighed dreamily as she looked around. It was one of the most beautiful rooms she had ever woken up in. The sumptuous fabrics and period furniture were combined with a classic elegance that somehow felt luxurious but not ostentatious. She thought of the en-suite bathroom and jumped out of bed eagerly. She was looking forward to a hot shower—something that would make a nice change from the lukewarm dribble that came out of the rusty showerhead at the chocolate shop.

Caitlyn smiled in anticipation as she padded barefoot into the en-suite. Maybe she'd even have a long bubble bath in that gorgeous clawfoot tub...

She stepped into the bathroom and nearly crashed into a sleeping old man, hanging upside down from the ceiling.

"*GAH!*" she cried, jumping out of her skin.

The old man opened one eye and squinted at her. "Eh? Who's that?" he mumbled sleepily.

"Viktor! What are you doing here?" demanded Caitlyn, trying to calm her racing heart. "You scared me half to death!"

The old man uncrossed his arms and stretched them above his head, almost touching the floor, as he yawned widely. Then he shuffled his feet—which seemed to be magically attached to the ceiling—and made an awkward attempt at a somersault. He wasn't quite successful, instead landing in a tangle of bony legs and arms on the floor.

"*Ahem.*" He picked himself up, his normally pale face slightly pink, and dusted his clothes off. As usual, he was wearing a black suit with a white ruffled shirt that looked like it had come straight out of an early nineteenth-century costume drama, and his few strands of grey hair had been meticulously combed across his balding head.

"Bloody uncomfortable, these ceilings," he muttered. "Not enough cobwebs to keep out the draughts..."

"Viktor, have you been in my bathroom all night?"

He gave Caitlyn an indignant look. "Of course. How else am I to protect you? I cannot have you staying in a strange house without me guarding your honour."

"Viktor...!" Caitlyn suppressed the urge to roll her eyes.

The old man scowled and wagged his finger at her. "I know what you are thinking, young lady. But don't underestimate your Uncle Viktor! I may be six hundred and thirty-four years old but I am still fighting fit! You haven't known fear until you have felt a vampire's teeth on your throat—*Yaaah!*"

He lunged at her, opening his eyes wide and pulling back his lips to bare his teeth. Caitlyn stared at the two gaps where his fangs should have been.

"Um... Viktor... where are your fangs?"

"Eh?" He faltered. Whirling, he hurried to the mirror above the vanity counter and peered into his sunken mouth. He gasped, "My fangs! They must have dropped out again! That cursed dentist! Utter moron! A pox of garlic on him!"

Muttering angrily, he bent over and began hunting around on the floor of the bathroom.

Caitlyn sighed and joined in the search, reflecting wryly that this was the other aspect of her new life that she was having trouble getting used to: having a shape-shifting vampire uncle. Especially since— based on the covers of all the romance novels Pomona liked to read—Caitlyn had always thought that shape-shifters were hunky men with rippling abs, ready to transform into snarling alpha wolves at the slightest provocation. But somehow *her* shape-shifter ended up being a decrepit old man who kept losing his teeth and turning into a fuzzy fruit bat.

"...must have dropped them in the greenhouse," Viktor muttered, climbing out of the shower cubicle empty-handed. "Hmm... could have been when I was trying to sample that pomegranate. Devilish tricky fruit, they are—lots of juice but getting through that tough outer skin is murder on my teeth..." He turned back to Caitlyn. "I shall have to return to the greenhouse to search for my fangs, once I have seen you safely back to the chocolate shop—"

"You don't need to worry about me," said Caitlyn in exasperation. "After all, this is Lord Fitzroy's home. Surely there can't be any place safer than Huntingdon Manor?"

"And yet someone was murdered here yesterday."

Caitlyn looked at him sharply. "You heard about that?"

"I may be old but I am not deaf," snapped Viktor.

He folded his arms and added loftily, "As it happens, the police have been parking their car under my favourite spot in the crabapple tree by the main driveway, and I have been privy to several of their conversations." He leaned close to Caitlyn and wagged a bony finger at her. "You be careful, young lady. That inspector has got you in his sights."

"Me? No, no, that was just a misunderstanding. I'm sure once Inspector Walsh speaks to Angela today, he'll see that I have a solid alibi—"

A sound at the bedroom door interrupted them. Caitlyn felt a flash of panic. What if someone came in and saw Viktor here? How was she ever going to explain what a strange old man was doing in her bedroom? She cringed as she imagined James's face.

"Stay here!" she hissed to the old vampire and hurried outside.

To her relief, she saw that the noise had come from a folded note being slipped under her door. She picked it up and read it. It was Pomona's handwriting:

Not sure whether to wake you or let you sleep, but if you're up, come down to breakfast in the Morning Room. See you there! xx

Caitlyn made sure the door was locked, then returned to the bathroom. "False alarm... but you'd better go, Viktor. I don't want to risk one of the staff coming in and seeing you..."

Viktor waved a dismissive hand. "Do not fear. I can instantly take my other form—"

"Yeah, well, I'm not sure finding a huge fruit bat in my bathroom would be any more reassuring," said Caitlyn. She hustled him out of the bathroom and led him over to the bedroom windows. "Please Viktor, you've got to go."

"Oh, very well," he said tetchily. "In any case, I have not had breakfast yet so I might as well—" He stopped as he caught Caitlyn's expression. "What?"

"Er..." Caitlyn swallowed. She had never given it much thought before but now it suddenly struck her what Viktor actually was. "You're... you're not going to go and suck someone's blood now, are you?"

Viktor bristled. "Excuse me, young lady! I find that a most offensive assumption!"

"Oh... sorry... I just thought that... with you being a vampire... you know..." Caitlyn trailed off helplessly.

"Just because we are vampires, it does not mean we are all the same," said Viktor huffily. "I'll have you know that I am a fruitarian, thank you very much! Those of us in the Megabat Order do not lower ourselves to something as sordid as drinking blood. Dis-gusting!" He flared his nostrils.

"A fruitarian?" Caitlyn laughed in relief. "Oh, right. Great. That sounds very... uh... healthy."

Viktor gave a disgruntled *harrumph*. Then he

stepped up to the windows and heaved one of the glass panes open. Caitlyn watched in amazement as the old man hunched forwards, seeming to fold in on himself, and then his body shrank and contorted, so that a moment later, where there had been a stooped old man, there was now a large fuzzy fruit bat. The creature climbed onto the windowsill, gave her a grumpy squeak over its shoulder, then launched itself out of the window and flapped away in the morning sunshine.

Caitlyn watched the bat flying away, wondering if she would ever get over seeing the shape-shifter transformation. Then she shut the window and hurried back to the bathroom. She looked wistfully for a moment at the deep enamelled bathtub. But no... If James and Pomona were already at breakfast, she didn't want to keep them waiting. Sighing, she grabbed a towel and turned towards the shower.

***

Twenty minutes later, with her hair still damp from the shower, Caitlyn found her way to the Morning Room and slid into a seat next to her cousin.

"Good morning," said James with a smile from across the table. "I hope you slept well?"

"Yes, thanks," said Caitlyn, giving him a shy smile in return.

"I thought you were never gonna come down, sleepyhead," said Pomona, munching on a piece of toast.

"Can I get you some tea or coffee?" asked James.

"Coffee, please. Black. One sugar," said Caitlyn. She inhaled gratefully as he handed her a steaming cup. There was nothing like the smell of fresh coffee in the morning.

"Now, what would you like?" James waved a hand towards the sideboard, which was bulging with serving platters. "You can have the full English... or you can just have a Continental breakfast if you prefer: rolls, pastries, preserves, orange juice..."

"Take the full English," said Pomona with her mouth full. "Trust me, it's worth it."

Caitlyn grinned. "All right. Hit me with it."

A short while later, Caitlyn wondered if she was going to regret her decision as she surveyed the enormous plate put in front of her. It was filled with fluffy scrambled eggs seasoned with fresh butter and chives, grilled tomatoes, sautéed mushrooms, strips of crispy bacon, fat juicy Cumberland sausages, and a puddle of baked beans, all accompanied by a rack of toast, carefully trimmed into triangular sections.

"I can't eat all this!" cried Caitlyn, staring at the overflowing plate. "There's enough food here for the entire British army!"

James laughed. "Just eat what you can. Leave

the rest."

"You'll eat everything, I promise," said Pomona with a smug smile as she popped the last piece of crispy bacon into her mouth. She sat back in her chair and rubbed her belly complacently. "Man, I have to say, when it comes to breakfast, the English sure know how to do it."

Caitlyn took a deep breath, picked up her knife and fork, and tackled the plate of food in front of her. She was surprised to find that, before she realised it, half the plate was gone. It was all so delicious, the different flavours and textures of the eggs, sausages, tomatoes, baked beans, mushrooms, and bacon somehow coming together to form the perfect combination in her mouth.

She was just accepting a second cup of coffee from James when there was a commotion in the hallway outside and, a minute later, several men entered the breakfast room. The first was Inspector Walsh and he inclined his head apologetically.

"Lord Fitzroy, Miss Le Fey, Miss Sinclair—I'm sorry to interrupt your breakfast..."

"Good morning, Inspector," said James, looking at him in surprise. "Would you like a cup of tea or coffee?"

"No, thank you, sir. I'm afraid I am here on business. Specifically, I need to ask Miss Le Fey a few more questions regarding her movements yesterday evening."

"Me?" Caitlyn looked up in surprise. Slowly, she

laid down her knife and fork as an uneasy feeling stole over her. She didn't like the inspector's grim expression and she couldn't help remembering Viktor's earlier warning.

"Is that really necessary, Inspector?" asked James, frowning. "Surely you ascertained last night that Miss Le Fey has an alibi for the time of the murder?"

"Ah, that is the very reason I need to speak to her again," said the inspector. He turned towards Caitlyn. "You told me yesterday, Miss Le Fey, that you were walking over the hill, back towards the chocolate shop, during the time the murder took place."

"Yes, that's right. "

"And you said that Angela Skinner would be able to confirm your story."

"Yes," said Caitlyn. "I met her just by the stone circle. Why?"

"I spoke to Miss Skinner this morning," said the inspector. "And she tells me that she never saw you yesterday afternoon." He leaned forwards and regarded Caitlyn grimly. "I hope, Miss Le Fey, you have not been lying to me."

CHAPTER SEVEN

"*What?*" Caitlyn stared at him. "What do you mean...? How could Angela say that? She *saw* me! We walked past each other—I even spoke to her!"

"What did you say?" asked the inspector.

"I... I said hello and made some small talk about the weather. I don't remember the exact words now."

"And what did Miss Skinner say in return?"

Caitlyn flushed and looked down. "Nothing. She... she snubbed me."

Pomona made an angry noise whilst James looked taken aback.

Inspector Walsh raised his eyebrows. "I see."

"But that doesn't mean she didn't see me," Caitlyn protested. "She definitely saw me! Even if she didn't speak to me—our eyes met and she deliberately turned away after I spoke to her."

"And why would she say that she didn't see you?" asked the inspector.

"Well, she—" Caitlyn broke off. She realised suddenly that Angela must have seen this as a perfect opportunity to get revenge, to make Caitlyn pay for some of the humiliation she had suffered. Angela was in a position of power here: Caitlyn's whole alibi rested on her verification. But how could she explain that to Inspector Walsh? Surely she couldn't tell him that the other woman had lied out of spite?

"Yes, Miss Le Fey?" asked Inspector Walsh.

Caitlyn squirmed. "I think she might be lying on purpose. There's... I think Angela is angry at me and this is a good way to get back at me."

The Inspector raised his eyebrows again and Caitlyn flushed even more. It all sounded so petty— like girls fighting in high school. Except that this wasn't a teenage popularity contest, thought Caitlyn grimly—this was a murder investigation and she was a prime suspect.

"Inspector, you're not seriously considering Caitlyn to be the murderer," said James in an incredulous tone. "I understand that her alibi may be unsubstantiated at present but there is no conceivable motive for her to hurt my housekeeper. They barely even knew each other. Surely there must be other more likely suspects?"

The inspector hesitated, then sighed and

conceded, "Yes, you are right, sir. We do have other suspects. But you will agree that I have to check every alibi."

"Naturally," James agreed. "I understand. But I think your time might be better spent following up the other suspects than hounding Miss Le Fey here."

"The thing is, Miss Le Fey was observed leaving the Manor in a furtive, hurried manner, just at the time the murder was likely to have happened, so you can see my difficulty, sir. We have to follow all leads." His tone changed. "And on that note, I also questioned one of your maids, Amelia, this morning. Miss Le Fey claims she overheard your housekeeper having an unpleasant scene with Amelia in her sitting room, not long before her murder."

"An unpleasant scene?" James looked at Caitlyn in surprise. "What about?"

Caitlyn shifted uncomfortably. It was obvious that James had no idea what his housekeeper was really like.

"Mrs Brixton was trying to blackmail Amelia," said Inspector Walsh bluntly.

"Blackmail!" James stared at him incredulously. "Mrs *Brixton*?"

"It has been confirmed by the maid herself," said the inspector. "Apparently, she was caught trying to steal something from the Library the day before the murder, and Mrs Brixton threatened to report the incident to you, unless Amelia paid her a regular sum from her wages."

James looked stunned. "This... this is incredible. I've known Mrs Brixton for years—she has been with my family ever since I was a little boy. I confess, I have never really liked her very much, but I had always thought her to be an upstanding, honest woman, if a bit cold and controlling at times." He frowned. "What was Amelia trying to steal?"

"A ring," said the inspector. "An antique signet ring with a dark red stone, which was kept in the display cabinet at the back of the Library."

"Oh, *that* ring," said James with a laugh.

"Is it valuable?" asked the inspector.

James shrugged. "It's never been valued by a jeweller, if that's what you're asking, but I doubt it's worth much in monetary terms; it isn't a precious jewel like a ruby. It's a bloodstone and its value—if you believe the legends—lies in its magical powers."

Pomona squealed in delight. "A bloodstone!" she said breathlessly. "Omigod, those are, like, one of the most mystical stones ever! They've got some *amazing* healing energy."

James gave a slightly sheepish smile. "Yes, I used to be fascinated by that ring when I was a boy. I spent hours in the Library, imagining all sorts of stories about it."

"What sort of stories?" asked Caitlyn.

James shrugged. "There are lots of legends attached to bloodstones. People in the Middle Ages believed they were formed at the crucifixion of Jesus Christ, when the blood of his wounds fell to the ground and turned to stone. And even before that, people in medieval times believed that they had the ability to stop blood flowing from any wound—which is why warriors used to carry bloodstone amulets to protect them in battle." He chuckled. "Lisa, my Marketing and Events Coordinator, is great at putting a romantic 'spin' on things and I think she found a book in the Library about bloodstones and decided to play up the ring's magical associations for the tourists' benefit. Makes a good story for the tour. But at the end of the day, it's all just folklore and superstition. It's just an old stone set in a ring—there's nothing magical about it."

Pomona opened her mouth, as if she might protest, then subsided again. Caitlyn knew that her cousin believed passionately in the occult and was always quick to defend the existence of magic, but this time, Pomona obviously felt it wasn't her place to argue with James. She couldn't resist adding, though:

"Well, Amelia obviously thought there was something magical about it, right? Otherwise, why would she have stolen it?"

"It seems that she wasn't stealing it for herself," said Inspector Walsh. "She claims that she received an anonymous note, saying that she would be paid a large sum of money if she extracted the ring from the Library. She was supposed to drop it off at a certain location in the Manor gardens, in return for the payment."

"Jeez, and she believed that?" Pomona rolled her eyes. "I mean, how did she know she'd get paid? Someone could have just gotten her to steal the ring for them, picked it up, and then run off without paying her a cent!"

The inspector gave a cynical smile. "People will believe anything they want to hear—especially when there is money involved."

"So what happened?" asked Caitlyn. "I mean, if Mrs Brixton caught Amelia red-handed, then she couldn't have made the drop-off, could she?"

The inspector nodded. "She left a note instead, explaining what had happened and that Mrs Brixton had confiscated the ring."

"You mean, the ring was in the housekeeper's possession when she was murdered?" asked Caitlyn.

The inspector gave her an admiring look again. "You are very quick, Miss Le Fey. Yes, the ring hadn't been returned to the Library—according to Amelia, Mrs Brixton still had it when they were having their 'discussion' yesterday afternoon... just before her murder."

"And she hasn't got it anymore?" asked Caitlyn.

"No, it wasn't found anywhere in her room or on her person."

"So are you saying that she could have been

murdered for the ring?" James spoke up.

"We are keeping an open mind at present," said Inspector Walsh. "But that is one working theory, yes. Whoever asked Amelia to steal the ring could have come to the Manor to speak to Mrs Brixton. Perhaps offer *her* payment in return for the ring. After all, we know now that the housekeeper liked money—she wasn't averse to using blackmail to line her pockets on the side—so it would be logical to assume that she might be open to negotiations. And perhaps those negotiations didn't quite go as planned..." He paused. "Of course, there is also another possibility—that it was *Amelia* who killed her and took the ring."

"Amelia?" said Caitlyn. "But... I saw Mrs Brixton after Amelia stormed out and she was fine."

"Ah, but she could have returned later, couldn't she?" said the inspector. "After all, we only have Amelia's word that she never went back to the housekeeper's sitting room yesterday evening. But she could easily be lying. And now she would have a double motive: not only would she get the ring and receive her payment, but she would also get rid of a woman who was threatening to blackmail her and make her life a misery."

"Omigod, yeah!" cried Pomona, wide-eyed. "You should arrest Amelia immediately!"

Inspector Walsh gave another cynical smile. "I'm afraid we British police are known for our slow and plodding nature, Miss Sinclair. We don't have the satisfaction of rushing in, guns blazing, to grab the fugitive—like the police do in Hollywood movies. We tend to ask a lot of pedantic questions and gather all the evidence we can before contemplating an arrest. Amelia Cole is certainly high on our list of suspects but, for the present, we are continuing with our investigation." He turned to James. "And now, Lord Fitzroy, I would like to interview another member of your staff: one of the gardeners—Matt O'Brien."

"Matt?" Pomona stiffened. "Why Matt?"

Inspector Walsh spoke to James. "My men have been interviewing the rest of your staff, Lord Fitzroy, and they reported that the other maid, Jenny, overheard an altercation between Mrs Brixton and Matt O'Brien the day before yesterday. Apparently, he was heard threatening her."

"Threatening her about what?" asked James.

"That is what I would like to find out," said the inspector. "I was planning to go and find Mr O'Brien now, to question him."

"I can ask him to come here, if you like," said James. "I would like to be present at the interview, if you don't mind, Inspector."

The inspector hesitated for a moment, then nodded. A few minutes later, the handsome Irishman was escorted into the Morning Room. Caitlyn noticed that he had lost none of his usual swagger and he stood at ease, a mocking smile on his face, as he faced the inspector.

"So what's this about, then?" he asked. "I hope it's important because I'm dealing with this fecking bat in the greenhouse! Keeps coming in to eat my nectarines—"

"We're conducting an investigation into Mrs Brixton's murder," said the inspector icily. "I should think that is far more important than a bat attacking your fruit trees, Mr O'Brien."

He shrugged. "So what do you want to ask me?"

"I understand that you had an argument with Mrs Brixton the day before she was killed?"

The gardener laughed easily. "Yeah, I had a bit of a bust-up with the old girl. But that was nothing new. We'd often have words. She was a right old bag—not to speak ill of the dead and all that," he added, not sounding respectful at all.

"So what was this specific argument about?"

"Well, Old Brixton was always coming down and sticking that big snout of hers where it don't belong. It's none of her business what I do in the greenhouse. I don't tell her how to fold the sheets, do I?"

The inspector didn't respond to Matt's grin. "That's all very well but you were heard threatening the housekeeper."

Matt gave another easy laugh. "Threatening her? They must have got the wrong end of the stick. I mean, I suppose things might have got a bit heated... I might have said a few things... you know how you do, when you're cheesed off. You don't really mean it."

"On the contrary, Mr O'Brien, I usually mean everything I say," said Inspector Walsh. "Especially when I say things like: *'if you don't keep your gob shut, I'll shut it for you for good'*. That sounds like an extreme reaction to a bit of disagreement over domestic matters, doesn't it?"

There was a pause, then Matt said, still in that easy, confident voice: "Like I said, Inspector, you say things sometimes in the heat of the moment. I've got a temper, all right? I admit that. It's the Irish in me. And Old Brixton could drive you mental sometimes with her whinging. I just wanted her to shut it."

The inspector changed tack. "I know my men have gone through this with you before but I'd like to ask you again—where were you last night between the times of seven fifteen and eight o'clock?"

"I was in the conservatory." Matt made a gesture towards Pomona, his lips curving up in a conspiratorial smile. "I was... uh... showing Miss Sinclair how to pinch the tips of the orange trees, to keep them full and bushy."

The inspector glanced at Pomona. "Do you corroborate that, Miss Sinclair?"

Pomona hesitated for a fraction of an instant. It was so brief that no one else would have noticed, not unless they knew her very well. But Caitlyn did. She looked at her cousin thoughtfully as Pomona raised her chin and said:

"Sure, Inspector. Matt was in the conservatory with me the whole time."

The Irishman smiled widely. Caitlyn tried to catch her cousin's eye but Pomona wouldn't look at her.

"Hmm… very well. That is all for now, Mr O'Brien," said the inspector.

The Irishman left the Morning Room, and a few minutes later, the police took their leave as well. Caitlyn looked back down at her plate. The food was cold now—but she had lost her appetite anyway. The earlier light-hearted mood at breakfast had completely gone. Even Pomona was subdued, fiddling with her napkin, her expression preoccupied.

James sighed. "I'm sorry about that. I understand that the police have to do their job but it can be unpleasant when they are questioning everyone."

Caitlyn felt a flash of sympathy for him. "It must have really disrupted your household since the murder yesterday. I mean, aside from the police being here, Mrs Brixton managed everything, didn't she?"

"Yes, she oversaw the running of the house and she also liaised with my Events Coordinator, Lisa, with regards to any events that the Manor was hosting. Luckily, we haven't got any bookings at the moment—the only big event coming up is the

Garden Party, which was supposed to be the day after tomorrow."

"Supposed to be? Are you cancelling it?" asked Caitlyn.

James ran a distracted hand through his hair. "I'm not sure. I did suggest it—out of respect for Mrs Brixton. I thought it would be wrong to have a party so soon after her murder. But so far, my suggestion hasn't been met with much enthusiasm. In fact, I'm quite surprised—most of the household staff don't seem to be as upset about her death as I would have expected. Nor the villagers I spoke to, either."

Caitlyn wasn't surprised in the least. The housekeeper had been a manipulative bully and she was sure that Mrs Brixton wasn't going to be mourned by many. Then she felt a stab of guilt. However bad the woman had been, she hadn't deserved to be murdered.

James sighed again. "I think I will probably let the Garden Party still go ahead. Which means— despite the police's insistence that the investigation comes first—I can't have staff just standing around, waiting to be questioned. The preparations for the party must be continued, especially as things will probably take even longer now without Mrs Brixton here to direct them."

They were interrupted by the sound of heavy paws and, a minute later, James's English mastiff, Bran, entered the Morning Room, accompanied by a little scrap of black fur.

"*Meew!*" cried the kitten, scampering up to Caitlyn's chair and attempting to climb up one leg.

"Hey there, sweetie..." Caitlyn reached down absently and picked up the kitten, settling him on her lap. The little cat snuggled against her, purring contentedly. The mastiff came lumbering over as well and shoved his jowly face into her lap too. Caitlyn laughed and patted his enormous head. "Yes, Bran... you too." She looked across the table at James and said regretfully, "I should really be getting back to the chocolate shop. The Widow Mags knew I was staying over but she might be getting worried now."

"I'll run you into the village in my car," James offered.

"I'll drive you," Pomona spoke up for the first time. She had been uncharacteristically quiet ever since the police left. Now she got up from her chair and made a great show of stretching. "I'd like to get some fresh air..."

"Have you got your car here?" asked Caitlyn, surprised.

"Yeah, James got them to bring it on the day they discharged me from the hospital."

"Oh." Caitlyn hesitated. To tell the truth, she wasn't that keen on going in Pomona's car. As was typical of her, her flamboyant cousin had rented the loudest, most eye-catching car possible—a bright red convertible—and her arrival in Tillyhenge last week had already caused a sensation. Caitlyn knew that—as a newcomer in the village—she was already the subject of avid curiosity and much gossip, and the last thing she needed was to call more attention to herself by riding back in Pomona's car. Still, it would have looked rude to reject her cousin's offer.

Caitlyn smiled wanly. "Uh... thanks. That'll be great." She lifted the kitten gently off her lap and set him back down on the floor.

"*Meew!*" cried the kitten, trying to climb back up into Caitlyn's lap.

"I think he'd like to go with you," said James with a chuckle.

"I'm sorry, sweetie," said Caitlyn. "You need to stay here—I can't take you to the chocolate shop."

"D'you need to get anything from your room?" Pomona asked, seeming suddenly impatient to leave.

Caitlyn shook her head. "No, I didn't bring a bag with me last night. What about you? Do you—"

"Nah, I've got my bag here," said Pomona, pointing to a large designer duffel bag lying on the floor next to her chair. "But gimme five minutes to go to the ladies', okay?"

CHAPTER EIGHT

"So what do you think of driving on the left side of the road?" Caitlyn said casually, glancing at Pomona.

Her cousin was staring straight ahead, frowning slightly at the windscreen, and was obviously in a world of her own. She hadn't said a word since they'd got in the car and left the Manor, which was strange in itself. Normally Pomona talked non-stop.

"Pomie, is everything okay?"

"Huh?" Pomona started, then looked guiltily at Caitlyn. "Oh, yeah..." She hesitated, then said, "Well, there was something... Nah, it's probably nothing."

"It's about Matt, isn't it?" Caitlyn asked.

Pomona gave her another guilty look. "How did you know?"

"I saw you hesitate when the inspector asked you to verify Matt's alibi."

"You did?" Her cousin looked alarmed.

"I don't think anyone else noticed," said Caitlyn. "It's only because I know you so well. But I'm right, aren't I? It's something about Matt—" She breathed in sharply. "He was lying, wasn't he? About being in the conservatory the whole time? And you covered up for him!"

Pomona winced. "Well... he put me on the spot! And I... I didn't wanna get him in trouble."

"Pomona!" Caitlyn cried in exasperation. "This isn't about getting someone in trouble—this is about finding a murderer!"

"But I know that Matt isn't the murderer!"

"How can you know that?"

"I just know, okay?" Pomona said. "I've got a good sense for this kind of thing. I mean, you know I'm slightly psychic. My mind, like, gets these vibes."

Caitlyn rolled her eyes. "Pomie... are you sure it's your mind and not some other part of your body getting the vibes? If Matt was a fat, old man instead of a sexy blue-eyed hunk, would you be covering for him?"

Pomona flushed. "You don't know him, Caitlyn! You haven't spent time with him, like I have. Matt just puts on this swaggering act, but underneath it all he's a really good guy."

"Well, okay, if he's got nothing to hide, why

doesn't he want to let the police know that he wasn't in the conservatory?" asked Caitlyn.

"'Cos they'd totally jump on him then," said Pomona quickly. "See, Matt's got a bit of a record— oh, nothing serious, just stuff he did when he was much younger—but it stays with you, doesn't it? In fact, he was having a hard time getting a job until James decided to give him a chance. But the police wouldn't care about all that. Matt said they've always been quick to go after him, and now they'd be looking for any excuse. And it's not like he was totally lying—he *was* with me in the conservatory for most of the time. He just went out for, like, ten minutes—to have a smoke, he said. But if it comes out that he doesn't have a solid alibi for the murder, the police would be all over him immediately." Pomona's bottom lip jutted out. "And they wouldn't give him a fair hearing. The police are already prejudiced against him to start with."

Caitlyn glanced warily at her cousin. It sounded like Matt had completely brainwashed Pomona and got her on his side.

"I'm saving the police time," continued Pomona blithely. "It's stupid for them to waste the effort going after Matt when he's not the murderer. They could use that time and energy to find the real killer."

"But what if Matt *is* the real killer?" burst out Caitlyn.

"He's not," insisted Pomona. "I know he's not.

81

You've gotta trust me."

"Look, if he really is innocent, then it won't matter if the police know. Let them investigate him and—"

"No!" said Pomona. "What if Matt loses his job? We can't—*Aaaiiihh!*"

She broke off and shrieked, and the car swerved wildly on the road.

"What? *What?*" cried Caitlyn.

"There!" Pomona pointed at her duffel bag, which had been dumped in the passenger-seat footwell next to Caitlyn's legs. "I saw something move in my bag!"

Caitlyn jerked her legs away from the bag and peered at it. Pomona was right—there was a bulge shifting and moving beneath the leather sides of the bag. She swallowed uneasily.

"Omigod, I read this story online about this woman who found a snake in her purse—like, a freaking python or something—and it slithered out and attacked her..." Pomona gabbled. "What if there's a snake in my bag? Maybe a cobra! Or a black mamba! They're, like, one of the most poisonous snakes in the world, right?"

"There are no black mambas in the Cotswolds," said Caitlyn shakily. "Or cobras, either. Anyway, how would a snake have got into your bag?"

"I don't know—it's moving! It's moving!" shrieked Pomona, pointing at the bag.

"Pull over!" said Caitlyn. "You're going to crash

and kill us before any snake gets us."

Pomona slowed down and pulled the convertible into a verge at the side of the road. As soon as the car stopped, the girls sprang out. Pomona hurried around to the passenger side and stood next to Caitlyn as both girls peered fearfully at the duffle bag.

"There! I just saw it move again!" cried Pomona, pointing wildly.

"What are we going to do?" asked Caitlyn. "We can't just stand here..."

"Maybe we should try and get it out. You know, prod the bag with something... like a stick..."

"And then what? Have the snake loose in the car? Or what if it gets out? We can't just leave a dangerous snake running loose in the countryside." Caitlyn looked at the fields around them. "We should call animal control or something like that."

"Yeah!" said Pomona. "Like those shows on TV! They must have forest rangers here in England too, right?" Then she made a face. "There's just one problem."

"What?"

"My phone's in my bag."

Caitlyn sighed and looked back into the car. Then she stiffened. "Pomie—I think... look, something's coming out!"

The two girls leaned closer and held their breath. Suddenly, something black and spiky popped out of the bag.

"AAAAAAHHH!"

"EEEEEIIIHHHH!"

Both girls screamed and jerked backwards, then they stared.

"Meew?"

Two big yellow eyes looked up at them as the little black kitten peeked its head out of the duffel bag.

"Omigod—it's the *cat!*" cried Pomona, clutching her heart.

Caitlyn started to laugh. She felt slightly hysterical. All the fear and tension turned into giggles and bubbled out of her mouth. After a moment, Pomona joined in and the two girls laughed until they were clutching their sides.

"Oh man..." Pomona gasped for a breath. "I think I just lost ten years off my life."

Caitlyn reached into the car and picked up the little kitten. "What are you doing here, you naughty thing?"

"Meew!" the kitten said cheekily. He looked with wide eyes at the open countryside around them and squirmed, as if trying to get down.

"Oh, no you don't," said Caitlyn, holding the kitten tighter and quickly getting back into the car. "You've caused enough trouble for one day."

Pomona got back in the driver's seat and re-buckled her seatbelt. "We're almost at the village," she said. "We can't go back to the Manor now. We'll have to keep him with us—and then I'll take him back with me later."

"Maybe I'd better put him back in your bag," said Caitlyn, as the kitten squirmed even more. "Otherwise, I'll never be able to keep hold of him while we're walking through the village."

"Hey! We can look for a cat carrier at the store in the village," suggested Pomona. "They seem to sell everything in there."

They drove into Tillyhenge a few minutes later and parked at the side of the village green, then followed Pomona's suggestion. Caitlyn had been in the village post shop a few times and it really did resemble Aladdin's cave, selling everything from toothpaste to tofu, tulips to telephone cards—as well as acting as the local post office. The only downside was that it also seemed to be Gossip Central in Tillyhenge and Caitlyn wondered if it was wise going in there now. She was uncomfortably aware of her own position as a suspect and knew that the villagers would like nothing better than to pump her for information about Mrs Brixton's murder.

Her worst fears were realised when they stepped in the shop and Caitlyn saw the usual group of gossiping women standing by the counter, presided over by the postmistress herself. They were watching the small TV mounted on a shelf behind the counter, where a news channel was playing. Caitlyn stopped short, wondering if the TV might be showing coverage of the murder, but, to her relief, it seemed to be a piece about a businessman who had been ruffling feathers by buying up large sections of the local countryside and turning the sites into modern developments.

"... representatives for Thane Blackmort have declined to comment but sources say that the reclusive billionaire is believed to be setting his sights on an area of wooded hills in the northern Cotswolds region..."

The women looked up as the two girls entered and their faces brightened. Caitlyn braced herself for the usual barrage of nosy questions. But she had forgotten that she was carrying a secret weapon: the kitten. The minute the women saw his little whiskered face, they forgot all about the girls; they surrounded Caitlyn, fussing and cooing over the baby cat.

"Where did you find him?"

"Look how small he is!"

"Needs a good feeding up, he does."

"Give him a mixture of evaporated milk mixed with cool boiled water, a teaspoon of glucose, and a small egg yolk. Works a treat every time."

"Yes, you've got to get the weight on him now, otherwise he might never catch up."

"Er... thank you," said Caitlyn, overwhelmed by this wealth of feline care information.

"Were you wanting to buy anything in particular

for the little mite?" asked the postmistress. "We do have some tinned cat food and a couple of boxes of the dried kibble but if you're after the special kitten formula, we don't stock that, I'm afraid."

"Actually, I was wondering if you might sell cat carriers?" Caitlyn looked at her hopefully.

The postmistress shook her head. "No, sorry, luv. I do sell a couple of collars and cat toys, but I'm not really a pet store. You'd have to go to one of the bigger towns around here."

"Oh... Okay, well, maybe I'll just get a collar for him then."

The postmistress pointed to the other corner of the store. "All the pet things are over there." She looked doubtfully at the kitten. "Might be hard to find something that will fit him though. What you can do is pick the smallest collar you can find and I'll help you add an extra hole, if you like."

"Thanks, that's really kind of you," said Caitlyn with a smile.

Pomona followed her to the other side of the store and they found a small nylon collar in lime green, with a bell attached. Back at the front counter, Caitlyn held the wriggling kitten while the postmistress measured his neck, then used a punching tool to add an extra hole for the buckle— whilst the rest of the women gathered around and watched and offered their opinions.

"There you go—that should keep him comfortable for a while, until he grows a bit bigger," said the postmistress, standing back and smiling with satisfaction.

"Hey, that lime green really suits him," said Pomona admiringly.

Caitlyn silently agreed with Pomona. The lime green of the collar stood out against the jet black of the kitten's fur and seemed to make his yellow eyes glow even more. He gave a little shake, causing the bell to tinkle, and Caitlyn laughed.

"Hopefully it'll be easier to keep track of where he is now," she said.

Pomona winked at Caitlyn. "Seriously, you've gotta let me give you a makeover. Even your cat is more stylish than you now."

CHAPTER NINE

They arrived back at *Bewitched by Chocolate* to find the Widow Mags sitting at her usual place behind the counter. Caitlyn was pleased to see a few tourists browsing in the store. Still not as many as she would have liked—it seemed a terrible shame that a shop selling such delicious chocolates should have such poor business—but it was an improvement on when she had first arrived.

A lot of that was down to Pomona, who had enthusiastically convinced the Widow Mags to let her do a "makeover" of the store last week, cleaning up the dusty shelves and creating a beautiful window display to tempt passers-by. The problem was, there weren't actually many passers-by. The chocolate shop was situated at the edge of the village and most of the villagers weren't that helpful about directing tourists down this lonely lane to find it. In fact, their prejudice against the Widow Mags because of her "witch" reputation made many of them seem to actively sabotage her business.

"What's that?" the Widow Mags demanded, pointing at Caitlyn's chest as the two girls approached the counter.

Caitlyn smiled as she held up the little black bundle. "It's a kitten I rescued in the woods last week. Lord Fitzroy has been looking after him at Huntingdon Manor but the little monkey managed to stow away in Pomona's bag."

"Well, I can't have him here, getting under everyone's feet," snapped the old woman.

"Pomona will take him with her when she goes back to the Manor, but in the meantime he won't be any bother," promised Caitlyn.

As she spoke, the kitten wriggled out of her grasp and dropped to the floor. He shook himself and immediately trotted off to explore his new surroundings, nearly tripping a tourist.

"Oh sorry!" cried Caitlyn as the man stopped himself crashing headlong into the counter just in time. She scooped up the kitten again and met the Widow Mags's accusing gaze.

"Put him in the kitchen," said the old woman. "At least he won't cause any accidents in there."

Caitlyn took the kitten into the back of the cottage and, after making sure that he had a soft blanket on one of the chairs to sleep on, left him happily romping about, exploring the kitchen. When she stepped back out into the front, she noticed a familiar face pressed against the shop window. It was the little girl from yesterday. This time she was looking wistfully down at the delectable chocolate truffles and bonbons laid out in the window display.

Caitlyn glanced over at the counter, where Pomona and the Widow Mags were busily engaged with a tourist, then walked over to the shop doorway.

Leaning out, she smiled at the little girl and said softly, "Hello."

The girl jerked back from the window and stared at her with huge, scared eyes, her hands clenched in fists at her sides.

"It's all right—I won't hurt you," said Caitlyn gently, crouching down so that she was more on the girl's level.

The little girl hesitated, shifting from foot to foot, as if deciding whether to run away.

"My name's Caitlyn—what's yours?"

The little girl stared at her. Then, in a tiny, almost inaudible voice, she whispered, "Molly."

Caitlyn smiled warmly. "That's a nice name. And how old are you, Molly? I'm twenty-two."

The little girl held up six fingers.

"Six?"

She nodded.

"Wow, you look really grown up for a six-year-old."

The little girl gave her a shy grin. She started to say something, then froze as they heard footsteps approaching the door from inside the shop. The next moment, the Widow Mags loomed in the doorway.

The girl gave a strangled cry, turned, and ran off down the lane as fast as her little chubby legs could carry her. Caitlyn sighed as she slowly stood up again and glanced surreptitiously at the old woman next to her. It was a shame that the Widow Mags looked so fearsome with her hooked nose, hunched posture, and hands gnarled by arthritis—unfortunately, she fit the stereotypical image of the "evil old witch" too perfectly!

The rest of the morning passed uneventfully, and after lunch, with no more customers in sight, the Widow Mags retreated to the kitchen. The two girls followed.

"Wow..." Pomona eyed the mountains of chocolate fudge piled in various trays on the wooden table. "That is a *serious* amount of fudge!"

"There's even more here than yesterday!" observed Caitlyn.

The Widow Mags looked slightly embarrassed. "Well, I didn't want Lord Fitzroy to go short."

"Can I taste one?" asked Pomona.

"In a minute. First, I want you girls to help me make some chocolate bars."

Pomona frowned. "I thought you just bought chocolate bars from the supermarket."

"Not *these* kinds of chocolate bars," said the Widow Mags with a smile. She nodded to Caitlyn. "Bring me a bowl of tempered chocolate."

Caitlyn hurried over to the large cauldron sitting in the hearth and ladled out some of the smooth melted chocolate into a smaller bowl. She took this over to the Widow Mags, who was standing at one end of the wooden table, surrounded by plastic moulds in an assortment of shapes and sizes.

"Take a few of the rectangular moulds each," the Widow Mags directed the girls. Then she pointed to several small bowls filled with different ingredients. "Sprinkle some of those in the bottom of each mould—different ones for each. Don't mix them up."

Pomona made an excited noise as the two girls stepped up to the table and began to work. Using her thumb and forefinger, Caitlyn picked up a pinch of roasted almond flakes from the first bowl and scattered that in the bottom of one of the moulds. Then she repeated it with the other moulds, using a pinch from each of the bowls: tangy candied orange, chopped pistachios, toasted coconut, crunchy toffee chunks, and a drizzle of salt flakes. Pomona was doing the same with different ingredients: roasted hazelnuts, tart red cranberries, tiny little marshmallows, brightly coloured M&Ms, and swirls of buttery caramel.

"Ooh, these look so delicious, I wanna try one right now!" said Pomona, licking a finger.

Caitlyn laughed. "We haven't even filled them

with chocolate yet."

The Widow Mags inspected their work and nodded with satisfaction, then she showed the girls how to pour melted chocolate into the moulds and scrape off the excess with a spatula.

"Make sure you give each mould a couple of good taps, once it's filled with chocolate, to ensure that there are no air bubbles," she instructed, rapping the spatula several times against the moulds to demonstrate. The melted chocolate shuddered and shifted in the hollowed-out sections, spreading evenly across from rim to rim.

"Now you try," said the Widow Mags.

Biting their lips in concentration, the two girls tried to copy her. It wasn't as easy as it looked! Melted chocolate kept going everywhere and they didn't have the Widow Mags's deft, experienced fingers. Still, although it took them a while, they finally stood back and proudly surveyed their work: all the moulds were filled with rich dark chocolate or creamy milk chocolate.

"Now what?" asked Pomona eagerly.

"Now we wait," said the Widow Mags. "We let them set. Because these are solid bars, the chocolate will take a while to cool down."

"Why don't we just put them in the fridge?"

"We can—but it's cool enough in that corner. I like to do things naturally, if I can." The Widow Mags waited until they had transferred the moulds to the corner to cool, then she beckoned them over with a smile. "While we're waiting, I will show you something to decorate the chocolate fudge cake I'm baking tomorrow for the party."

She picked a new mould—this time in the shape of a butterfly—and brought it near the bowl of tempered chocolate. But instead of filling up the mould completely with chocolate, she used the spatula to drizzle a thin trickle of the melted chocolate across the inner surface, so that it formed a sort of filigree pattern across the shape of the butterfly.

This time the thin chocolate layer cooled and set quickly and, after a few minutes, the Widow Mags turned the mould over and gave it a gentle tap. A delicate chocolate butterfly fell into her open palm. She laid it carefully on a piece of wax paper, and the delicate swirls that made up its wings almost looked like chocolate gossamer.

"That's beautiful," breathed Caitlyn.

"Yeah, it's like magic!" said Pomona.

The Widow Mags gave a raspy chuckle. "Oh no... *this* is magic." Reaching out a hand, she touched the butterfly with her forefinger and chanted softly:

Dormant creature,
Of magic partake;
Heed my words,
Arise and awake!

The two girls watched in amazement as the

chocolate butterfly suddenly trembled, then the two wings lifted slowly, folding until they touched together at the top. Then they unfolded and lowered again. Folded and unfolded. Folded and unfolded. The next moment, the chocolate butterfly took flight, transforming somehow into a real butterfly as it rose up from the wooden table.

"Omigod..." Pomona whispered, watching open-mouthed as the butterfly fluttered around the kitchen.

Caitlyn put out a hand and the butterfly landed on her finger. She stared at it in wonderment. Its wings were a beautiful dark brown, with creamy swirls in a pattern that somehow resembled the chocolate filigree... but it was real, not made of chocolate.

"You brought it to life!" she said, looking at the Widow Mags in awe.

The Widow Mags handed her the spatula. "Now you try."

"Me?" Caitlyn was taken aback. "Well, I can make a chocolate butterfly but I can't enchant it and bring it to life—"

"Yes, you can." The Widow Mags looked at her intently. "You are a witch."

Caitlyn swallowed. She took the spatula and copied the Widow Mags's movements, drizzling the melted chocolate onto the inner surface of the mould and letting it set, then turning it over to tap out a delicate chocolate butterfly. She laid this nervously on the wax paper and looked at the Widow Mags.

"I... I don't know the words."

"The power of the spell is not in the words themselves; magic is simply the ability to cause change by force of will. The spell works because you will it to, with your mind. However—" the old woman conceded, "—as humans are verbal creatures, spoken words help you to have something to focus your mind on, especially when you are young and inexperienced."

She repeated the words of the spell and Caitlyn said it silently in her head. Then she took a deep breath and chanted the same words that the Widow Mags had said. Pomona leaned forward eagerly, staring at the chocolate butterfly on the table.

Nothing happened.

"Try again," said the Widow Mags.

Caitlyn took another breath and said the spell again. This time, she thought she saw the wings of the butterfly tremble—ever so slightly—then the illusion was gone, and it was once more just a dainty piece of chocolate sitting on a piece of baking paper. Caitlyn felt a deep stab of disappointment.

"I can't do it!" she burst out. "I *knew* I wouldn't be able to bring it to life."

The Widow Mags gave her a long look. "*That...* is why you failed."

CHAPTER TEN

The rest of the afternoon passed in a blur. By the time the Widow Mags declared that they were done for the day, Caitlyn and Pomona were both smeared with chocolate and slightly high from all the sweet cocoa treats they had consumed.

"I think I'd better head back to the Manor now," said Pomona reluctantly, taking off her apron. She scanned the room. "Where's the kitten?"

Caitlyn looked around in surprise. The kitten had been scampering about, pouncing and stalking around their feet as they worked, and she thought he was still there, playing under the table.

She frowned. "I don't see him anywhere. Do you think he might have got out? We've kept the door of the kitchen shut—"

"He's here on my lap," the Widow Mags spoke

up.

Both girls stared at her in surprise, then leaned over to look under the table. Yes, there he was, the little black kitten, curled up in the old witch's lap, sleeping soundly.

"Aww, he looks so sweet," said Pomona. "Shame I have to wake him up."

"You can leave him," said the Widow Mags gruffly. "He can stay the night if he likes."

The girls exchanged startled looks. This was a change of tune! Caitlyn hid a smile. It looked like the little kitten had won even the cantankerous Widow Mags over!

"Have you decided what you're gonna call him?" Pomona asked Caitlyn.

She shook her head helplessly. "I have no idea. I mean, I suppose I could go with one of the usual names for black cats... Sooty? Inky? Jet? Blackie?"

"Nibs," said the Widow Mags suddenly. "That's what he reminds me of. Cocoa nibs. Dark and tiny but packing a punch in flavour."

"Nibs," repeated Caitlyn, a slow smile spreading across her face. "Yeah, it suits him!" She looked at Pomona. "Tell James I'll bring Nibs back to the Manor tomorrow."

* * *

Caitlyn and the Widow Mags had just finished an early supper when they heard the sound of footsteps at the back door and, a minute later, a middle-aged lady wearing a voluminous purple kaftan and a matching purple turban atop her frizzy red hair came bustling into the kitchen. She was followed by a lanky teenage girl of about eighteen, with similarly frizzy hair and an eager smile.

"Caitlyn! How nice to see you, dear," said Bertha. She surveyed the chocolate pieces laid out across the table. "My, I see that you have been busy, Mother. Is this all for the Garden Party?" She blinked. "Don't you think you've made a bit too much?"

"Better too much than too little," said the Widow Mags. She looked at the girl and waved a hand at the trays of fudge. "Have some fudge, Evie."

"The dark chocolate caramel is amazing," Caitlyn said as the girl hesitated over which flavour to choose. "Although Pomona thinks the peanut butter swirl is the best."

"Pomona's here?" asked Evie, looking around eagerly.

"She was but she went back to the Manor a couple of hours ago."

Caitlyn smiled inwardly as she saw Evie's face drop. In the short time since Evie had known Pomona, the teenage girl had developed a serious case of hero-worship and most of her conversation now centred around what Pomona wore and what Pomona said. In fact, she was wearing a large satin flower in her frizzy hair now, in a slavish imitation of the way Pomona wore hers—except without the same aplomb, since Evie kept fiddling self-consciously with hers. The thing most people didn't realise was that Pomona looked gorgeous not so much because of the outrageous things she wore but because of the confidence with which she wore them.

"Are you ready, Mother?" asked Bertha, glancing at her watch. "We don't want to be late."

"All right, all right—don't fuss," said the Widow Mags, rising from the table. She placed the sleeping kitten gently onto a folded blanket nearby. "I don't see why I have to keep doing this anyway," she grumbled.

"Mother, you know why—the physiotherapy is good for your arthritis." Bertha came to stand behind her mother and draped a shawl around her shoulders.

The Widow Mags twitched irritably. "What do I need a shawl for? It's the middle of summer!"

"It's quite chilly outside, Mother. I had goosebumps as soon as I stepped out—"

"I don't feel cold. Just because you do, doesn't mean that I will too," said the Widow Mags. She pushed the shawl off her shoulders. "Anyway, I would rather wear my own cardigan. I just need to remember where I put it—"

"I'll help you look for it, Grandma," Evie offered and left the kitchen with the old woman.

As soon as they were alone, Caitlyn glanced

quickly around, then sidled up to Bertha and said:

"Bertha—have you got a moment? I need to ask you something."

Bertha looked at her in surprise. "Yes, dear?"

Caitlyn reached under the collar of her T-shirt and pulled out her runestone. "Last week, when I was asking you about this, you started to tell me about your own runestone—"

"Caitlyn..." Bertha looked uncomfortable. "I can't talk about this."

"Why? Please, Bertha—this is really important to me! I need to know. Why do you have the same runestone that I have?"

Bertha shifted uncomfortably, looking torn. "Do you know where yours came from?" she asked at last, evading the question.

Caitlyn shook her head. "I only know that it was around my neck when I was found as a baby—very near Tillyhenge actually. My adoptive mother found me; she was being driven to some country house party and they were forced to go on a detour down a country lane for some reason, and that's when she found me. I was only a few hours old, so I must have been born in this area." Caitlyn leaned forwards and looked at the other woman earnestly. "That's the reason I came to Tillyhenge, you know. I think my mother—my family—might have come from around here."

Bertha hesitated for a long moment. She touched a hand to her throat, where her own runestone hung on a length of ribbon, and sighed. Then she said, "I was given this runestone as a little girl... well, it's actually half of a runestone. My sister had the other half."

"Your sister? You have a sister?"

Bertha nodded slowly and a dreamy look came into her eyes. "Yes, she was ten years younger than me and so beautiful... You could tell, even when she was a toddler, that she was going to be a great witch someday. She just had that innate gift, that special quality..." She trailed off sadly.

"What happened to her?" Caitlyn was almost afraid to ask.

Bertha hesitated again. "She—" She broke off as they heard footsteps coming back towards the kitchen. "Ah great, you're ready!" she said brightly as the Widow Mags and Evie came back into the room. "Well, we'd better dash now! See you later, girls—be good!"

Looking almost relieved, Bertha hustled the Widow Mags out of the back door and slammed it behind them. Caitlyn heaved a sigh of frustration. Why couldn't she ever get answers from Bertha? Then her eyes fell on Evie and she felt a surge of hope. Maybe if the mother couldn't tell her, the daughter would...

"Hey, Evie," she said casually. "Do you have a big family?"

The girl shook her head and smiled. "No, just Mum and me."

"Oh." Caitlyn wondered if Bertha was a single mother and felt too embarrassed to ask for more details. "So... um... you don't have any aunts or uncles?"

Evie shook her head again.

"Your mother was an only child too?"

Evie frowned. "I guess so. She never talks about a brother or sister—and neither does Grandma."

"So no cousins at all?"

"No," said Evie wistfully. She gave Caitlyn a smile. "I wish I had a cousin like Pomona."

"What about any other family?" asked Caitlyn desperately.

Evie shrugged. "I guess we must have other family but Mum never talks about them. In fact, now that you mention it, it is a bit weird that Mum and Grandma never talk about that kind of stuff. You're making me curious now... Hey, I know! Maybe there would be pictures in Grandma's photo album."

"Photo album?"

Evie nodded. "She has a big, old-fashioned one. I remember seeing it when I was younger. She keeps it somewhere in her bedroom. Come on, let's go and look—" She hurried from the kitchen.

Caitlyn followed her and hovered uncertainly in the doorway of the Widow Mags's bedroom. "Um... are you sure we should be doing this? I mean, your grandmother's not going to be happy that we're snooping in her bedroom."

Evie hesitated, then she grinned at Caitlyn over her shoulder. "But she doesn't have to know, does she? They'll be at least an hour at the physio—if we hurry, we'll be able to find the album, look through it, and put it back, before they get back."

"All right." Caitlyn followed her into the bedroom, her reluctance and guilt about invading the Widow Mags's private space warring with her desire to find information. "Where do we start?"

Now that they were in the room, Evie looked uncertain. "I don't know..."

Caitlyn glanced around. It was a large room with an old oak bed dominating one side and a small sitting area on the other side, consisting of an ancient writing desk, a couple of armchairs, and a sagging couch. An enormous chest of drawers stood against one wall, with a huge old-fashioned wardrobe next to it. There was also a bookshelf on the other wall and several boxes, trunks, and chests piled in the corners of the room. Caitlyn's heart sank. It would take them hours to go through everything.

Then her eyes alighted on the bedside table, which had a cabinet door underneath. She crossed over to it and Evie followed her eagerly.

"Do you think the album might be in there?" she asked.

Caitlyn shrugged. "People tend to keep their personal items near their bed, don't they?"

"Yeah, that's a good idea!"

Evie opened the cabinet door, then knelt down beside it and rummaged inside. She emerged a few minutes later triumphantly brandishing a large, leather-bound volume. Caitlyn's heart leapt. She peered over Evie's shoulder as the girl eagerly opened the album.

They both stared in disappointment. There were no photos inside. The pages were completely bare.

"That's weird!" said Evie, frowning as she flipped through the yellowed pages. "I'm sure this was the album I saw before—and it was full of pictures!"

"Do you think your grandmother removed all the photos?" asked Caitlyn.

"Maybe... but then why keep the empty album?"

"Maybe she wants to use it again."

Evie was silent for a minute, then she looked up at Caitlyn excitedly. "No, I think it's an enchanted album!"

"An enchanted album?"

Evie nodded eagerly. "There's a spell on it. Grandma must have done it, to protect it from people snooping. The photos are all there, but you just can't see them. But don't worry," she added blithely. "I know how to unlock the spell."

"Er... are you sure?" asked Caitlyn nervously. She'd experienced some of Evie's attempts at casting spells and they usually ended in disaster. Her hand went reflexively to her forehead and she touched her eyebrows to reassure herself that they were still normal.

"Oh yes," said Evie loftily. "It's a doddle."

She held the album up in front of her and raised a hand, waving her fingers over it. Then she screwed up her eyes and muttered, "*Manifesto ex privatus!*"

There was a faint hum, then a sharp crackling sound, and something sparked from Evie's fingertips. A gust of wind *whooshed* around them and Caitlyn felt her hair lift up around her head, then settle back down again around her shoulders.

Hastily, she touched her forehead again to make sure her eyebrows were still in place. Then she froze and looked down at herself. She blinked, wondering if she was seeing things. No, it was true. She was wearing her bra and panties on the *outside* of her clothes. She looked at Evie and saw that the teenage girl was also wearing her underwear over her T-shirt and jeans. The two of them looked like a pair of bizarre superheroes.

"What did you do?" she asked Evie.

"Sorry..." Evie mumbled, looking embarrassed. "It's just a small mistake. I must have remembered the words wrong." She smiled and held up her hand again. "Okay, not to worry. What I need is to show what's *underneath,* not what's *private—*"

"Wait, Evie," said Caitlyn quickly. "Maybe this isn't such a good idea—"

"Don't worry, I know what I'm doing," said Evie confidently. She waved her fingers and said, "*Subtus manifesto!*"

There was another *whoosh* of air, this time followed by a terrible cracking sound beneath their feet. Caitlyn felt the floorboards tilt beneath her and stumbled sideways, nearly falling over. She looked down and stifled a scream.

An enormous gnarled root had thrust its way up through the cracked floorboards and was flicking around, like a giant brown tentacle. All around the room, more roots were pushing up through the floorboards, bristling with soil and hairs.

Evie shrieked and stared around the room, wide-eyed. "*Oh my Goddess!*"

"Stop it, Evie! Stop it, whatever you're doing!" cried Caitlyn

"I don't know what I'm doing!" said Evie desperately. "I thought that *was* the right spell. I thought... I was getting the things underneath to rise up and show themselves..."

"Well, the wrong things are rising up and showing themselves!" said Caitlyn as she stumbled backwards away from a long brown root that was slithering its way across the floor.

"What should I do?" asked Evie shrilly.

"You're asking *me*?" said Caitlyn. "You're the one who's the witch!"

"You're a witch too!" Evie retorted.

"Well... most of my training so far has been about making enchanted chocolates. I haven't got to the bit about how to control monster roots!" Caitlyn looked around frantically. More and more roots were shooting up through the floorboards and several of them were growing larger and larger, unfurling and twisting up towards the ceiling. Pretty soon, the entire room would be filled with giant roots growing upwards. She wondered what would happen when the roots encountered the ceiling— would they push through that too? And the roof? If they kept growing like this, the whole cottage could be destroyed.

"We've got to do something!" she said. "Isn't there... like... an 'UNDO' button for magic?"

"Oh! Yes! Yes, there is!" cried Evie, her face brightening. "Grandma taught me this. She said if I ever messed up, I could always use this to reverse any spell." She screwed up her eyes again and mumbled, "Let me see if I can remember it..."

Caitlyn held her breath, trying to resist the urge to hurry the girl. Evie opened her eyes and took a deep breath, then chanted:

What's done cannot be undone,
But now this mess is begun;
Make it go back,
Back make it go;
Just as it was,
And no one will know!

For a moment, nothing happened, then suddenly, as if by magic—and it was!—the roots vanished. The wooden floor was back to normal again, smooth and intact, and Caitlyn and Evie were standing in the middle of the room, breathing hard and staring at each other.

"I think we should put this back now," said Caitlyn shakily, reaching to grab the photo album. "We don't need any more disastrous spells-gone-wrong." She paused as she saw the crestfallen expression on Evie's face and felt a pang of pity for the girl.

"Hey..." She reached out and patted Evie's arm. "You gave it a good try. It was probably too hard a spell to break."

"No, it's not that—I'm just a rubbish witch," said Evie in small voice, her shoulders slumping.

"No, you're not," said Caitlyn quickly. "I'm sure you're going to be a great witch! Everyone makes mistakes when they're learning. I'm sure witchcraft is just like any other skill—like drawing or playing the piano—you have to practice to get good at it."

"Some people don't," said Evie wistfully. "Some people are born just able to draw beautifully, aren't they? Or play an instrument or sing..."

"Yeah, I guess... But I'll bet even they have to practice. And besides, most people who look like they have amazing abilities... well, I'm sure they've mostly got there by hard work, not just natural talent." Caitlyn hesitated, then, against her better judgement, said, "Do you... do you want to give it another go?"

Evie looked gratefully at her and nodded. She

closed her eyes for a second, frowning in concentration, then took a deep breath, pointed at the album, and whispered, "*Manifesto clandestina!*"

A puff of smoke rose from the album and Caitlyn gasped, thinking that they'd set it on fire. Then, to her surprise and delight, she saw photographs start to appear on the pages.

"You did it!" she cried.

Evie opened her eyes and a wide smile spread across her face as she stared at the photos being revealed. "Oh my Goddess—it worked! I did it!"

Caitlyn leaned eagerly over the album and turned the pages. She froze almost immediately as she saw a large photograph in the centre of the album. It showed a stern-faced woman with dark hair pulled back in a messy bun, dressed in clothes that were from the late 70s or early 80s. With a shock, Caitlyn realised that it was the Widow Mags as a much younger woman.

There were two young girls standing on either side of the Widow Mags, each holding her hand. One was a teenage girl of about fourteen and the other was probably around four years old, barely more than a toddler. The older girl looked familiar— in fact, Caitlyn realised, she looked a lot like Evie. But it was the little girl who drew her eye. Caitlyn felt her heart constrict as she peered closely at the photograph.

The girl looked eerily like her.

CHAPTER ELEVEN

Caitlyn stared at the photograph, her thoughts whirling. She remembered seeing photos of herself as a young child—pictures Barbara Le Fey had taken of her at the beach, eating an ice-cream, trying to play the guitar... The little girl in this photo, with her vivid red hair, wide hazel eyes, and the smattering of freckles across her nose and cheeks, looked incredibly similar to her at the same age.

But Caitlyn knew this wasn't her. So who was she? And the other girl... Suddenly, Caitlyn realised that the older girl must have been Bertha as a teenager. Yes, even then, she was dressed all in purple, in a violet tie-dye dress with purple sandals.

"Is that...? Oh my Goddess, that's Mum!" cried Evie, giggling as she looked at the picture. "Look what she's wearing! And that must be Grandma... but who's the little girl—?"

They both jerked their heads up as they heard the faint sound of voices outside.

"They're back!" hissed Evie.

She slammed the album shut and shoved it back into the bedside cabinet. Then the two of them scrambled to get out of the bedroom. They managed to step out and slam the door behind them just as Bertha and the Widow Mags walked in.

"Evie? Caitlyn?" Bertha stared at them in astonishment. "What on earth have you girls been up to?"

Caitlyn followed the direction of Bertha's gaze and looked down at herself. She groaned inwardly. They had completely forgotten about their underwear, which was still being worn on top of their clothes!

"Er... I was just showing Evie some of the latest fashion trends in Hollywood," said Caitlyn glibly. "Innerwear as outerwear! It's all the rage at the moment."

Bertha looked at her doubtfully. "People wear their bras and knickers on the outside in Hollywood?"

"Innerwear as outerwear? I've never heard such nonsense," the Widow Mags snapped.

Caitlyn was relieved that Bertha and Evie left soon after and she could retreat to her attic bedroom. She wanted time alone to think. She couldn't get her mind off the photo she had seen in the album. Bertha had talked about having a younger sister... so was that little girl in the photo the Widow Mags's other daughter? And why did she look so much like Caitlyn as a child? Pomona had suggested that Bertha was her aunt and the Widow Mags her grandmother... If that was true, then was that little girl her mother?

Caitlyn felt a tingle of excitement. Was she making some progress at last? She had come to Tillyhenge looking for answers about her family and her past, and she had certainly found out some things she hadn't expected—such as discovering that she was a witch!—but the questions about her real mother and her family had remained unanswered... until now. Caitlyn smiled suddenly to herself. If this was true, then it would mean that her family had been right here all along, under her very nose!

She turned over in the narrow bed, the springs creaking under her weight, and sighed. But if this was true, why hadn't they said anything? Why hadn't they recognised her and claimed her as family? Surely they must have seen her resemblance to her mother? Caitlyn frowned as she thought back to her first meeting with Bertha in her store, *Herbal Enchantments*—she remembered the older woman looking at her strangely and saying that Caitlyn reminded her of someone... The Widow Mags too, although she had never come out and said anything, had often looked at her with a speculative intensity which Caitlyn found slightly disturbing.

But why hadn't they said anything? Why wouldn't they talk about her mother? And where was that little girl in the photograph now?

***

When Caitlyn woke up the next morning, she was surprised to feel a warm furry bundle nestled against her neck. She shifted slightly and turned her head to look, then smiled as she saw the little black feline face with the dainty whiskers. Oh yes, of course... the kitten had spent the night with her. He stirred as she moved and opened his mouth, displaying a small pink tongue and tiny sharp teeth.

"*Meew?*" Nibs said sleepily, looking up at her.

Caitlyn reached over to tickle him under the chin and the little kitten began to purr loudly. Caitlyn smiled again. There was something lovely about waking up with a warm, sleeping cat curled up against you.

Better not get used to it, she thought to herself as she jumped out of bed. She would have to return Nibs to the Manor today. The kitten got up as well and arched his back in a perfect little cat stretch, then hopped off the bed and trotted over to the bedroom door.

"*Meew!*" he said, looking expectantly back at Caitlyn.

She chuckled. "Not even two pounds and you're bossing people around already!"

***

An hour later, Caitlyn parked her rented Volkswagen Beetle at the side of the gravel driveway which circled the front of Huntingdon Manor, picked up the kitten in her arms, and got out of the car. There was a hive of activity around her as staff hurried to and fro, setting up the tables, testing the sound systems, placing cushions on the chairs, arranging the flower displays, and draping the bunting across the tree branches for the Garden Party tomorrow.

"*Meew!*" cried the kitten excitedly as he recognised the familiar surroundings. He wriggled wildly in her arms, trying to get free.

Caitlyn hesitated. She wasn't sure it was a good idea to set Nibs down here on the front lawns—he might trip one of the staff or get squashed by equipment or have some other accident. She would take him into the house before she released him, she decided.

Keeping a firm grip on the squirming kitten, Caitlyn walked up to the front entrance, but as she was starting up the steps, she saw two men struggling to carry a trestle table coming through the front doors. She darted quickly out of their way, and then, on an impulse, turned and took the path which led around the side of the Manor. There was a side door here that she remembered seeing. She found it easily, tucked between two hydrangea bushes, and was relieved to find it unlocked. Stepping through, she found herself in a small hallway with several doors leading off from it. She frowned, trying to remember the orientation of the Manor and where this hallway was in relation to the main rooms. The kitten gave a violent wriggle and jumped out of her grasp.

"Nibs!" she gasped, making a lunge to grab the little cat.

He evaded her easily and trotted over to the nearest door, which was slightly ajar.

"Nibs—come back here!" Caitlyn cajoled.

"*Meew!*" the black kitten said cheekily, then turned and darted into the room.

"*Nibs!*" Caitlyn hurried after the little cat and poked her head into the room, looking nervously around.

It looked like some kind of office, with a large antique writing desk in one corner and filing cabinets along one wall. Like all rooms in the Manor, though, it still retained its period features and a sense of luxurious elegance; in this case, enhanced by a beautiful black lacquered Chinese screen—with ornate panels decorated with mother-of-pearl—which stood along the far wall.

Caitlyn hesitated. She felt guilty entering what was obviously a private office uninvited. On the other hand, she didn't like just leaving the kitten loose in there either. What if someone came along and locked the door and poor Nibs was stuck in the office for days? She had to find him.

She stepped into the room and peered around. "Nibs? Nibs, where are you?"

There came a faint "*Meew!*" from the far corner, by the antique writing desk.

Caitlyn took a few more steps into the room. "Nibs? Come out, you little monkey!"

She saw a ball of black fluff scamper across the corner and disappear under the desk.

"Nibs!" she hissed, hurrying across the room to the desk.

When she reached it, the kitten was nowhere in sight. Caitlyn bent over to look in the cut-out space beneath the desk. She wished now that she had taken the time to switch on the lights in the room— it was dark in this corner and she could barely see into the black kneehole beneath the desk.

"Nibs?" she whispered. She reached a hand into the black hole and groped around.

"*Meew!*" The kitten was definitely in there but trying to see a black cat in a black hole was an impossible feat.

Caitlyn hesitated, then sighed and got down to crawl on all fours into the kneehole under the desk. The opening was narrow and with her hips blocking out most of the light, it was pitch black in there. She couldn't do anything but grope blindly around, hoping to find the kitten.

"Nibs...?"

Suddenly she felt the floor shaking and, the next moment, she heard what sounded like heavy footsteps entering the room. Then something warm and furry shoved her hips aside and pushed its way into the space beneath the desk. Caitlyn felt something cold and wet touch her arm and heard the sound of loud sniffing.

She nearly yelped with fright before she realised that the cold, wet thing was a very big doggie nose and the warm, furry "invader" was the huge mastiff's head.

"Bran!" she said in exasperation, trying to turn around in the small space. "Don't do that! You scared me half to death!"

"*WOOF!*" said the big dog. He bent down and began trying to climb into the narrow space with her.

"Wait, Bran—you can't come in here too! There isn't enough space for both of us!" protested Caitlyn, bracing her hands against the huge mastiff to try and stop him advancing. It was like trying to stop a furry steamroller. Then she tried to wriggle out past him but found that she was now wedged against the back of the kneehole, with the dog's body blocking the way out. She shoved uselessly at him again. "Bran—you've got to move!"

"*WOOF!*" said Bran joyfully, as he somehow managed to curl his enormous body into the space in the kneehole next to her.

"*Meew!*" The kitten suddenly popped up from under Caitlyn's armpit. He crawled into her lap and curled up there.

The mastiff wagged his tail with delight at seeing his little friend and it whacked against the side of the desk, sending shuddering spasms through the wood with each impact.

THUMP! THUMP! THUMP!

Bran panted happily in time to his wagging tail and drooled on Caitlyn's shoulder.

This cannot be happening to me, she thought. She was being held hostage, squashed in a corner of a desk kneehole, with a giant slobbery dog and a kitten in her lap...

The next minute, the lights went on in the room and Caitlyn groaned inwardly as she saw a pair of smart Italian men's shoes cross the floor and come towards her. James Fitzroy's face appeared in the gap of the kneehole and he stared at her in astonishment.

"Caitlyn? What on earth are you doing there?"

CHAPTER TWELVE

Caitlyn opened her mouth to explain, then gave up. "Just help me out, please," she begged.

James chuckled and gave Bran a shove. "Come on, Bran. Get out of there—come on! Good boy!"

The mastiff heaved himself slowly to his feet and backed carefully out of the hole, reminding Caitlyn of a huge double decker bus reversing. She crawled gratefully out in his wake and accepted James's hand as he reached down to help her to her feet.

"What on earth were you doing in there?" he repeated, a smile hovering at the edge of his lips.

"I was looking for the kitten—"

As if on cue, a furry little black face peeked suddenly out of the kneehole. "*Meew!*"

"Ah, you brought him back," said James with a smile of relief. "Thank goodness. Bran has been pacing around the house, whining and looking for his little friend." He shook his head and laughed. "You won't believe the drama that kitten has caused. The whole house was frantic yesterday when it was discovered that he was missing—I was almost about to send out a search party, when Pomona came back and told us that he was with you."

"Sorry!" said Caitlyn. "I should have thought of calling you and letting you know. Nibs stowed away in Pomona's bag and we didn't even realise it until we were almost at the village."

"Nibs?"

"That's what I've decided to call him," said Caitlyn shyly. "From cocoa nibs. You know, those small, dark, crunchy pieces of cacao bean, full of intense chocolatey flavour. It was the Widow Mags who came up with it—she thought it suited him. He's only a little scrap of fur, but boy, he makes up for it with tons of personality. Tiny but powerful."

James laughed. "It does suit him, indeed. All right, Nibs it is. I hope he wasn't too much of a nuisance at the chocolate shop."

"No, in fact, I think the Widow Mags is quite smitten with him—not that she would ever admit it, of course," said Caitlyn with a chuckle. "But she was the one who suggested that he should stay the night."

"Did he sleep with her?" said James in disbelief.

"No, he spent the night cuddled up in bed with

me."

"Lucky kitten."

Caitlyn glanced quickly at him, startled. Surely he couldn't have meant what she thought he meant...? She felt a blush begin to heat her cheeks, then James added:

"He could have had a very bad adventure, if you hadn't found him in time and kept him safe."

"Oh! Y-yes, of course, h-he was very lucky," stammered Caitlyn, now blushing for a different reason. She was embarrassed at her own assumption. How could she have thought that James meant those words in any other way? That would have suggested that he was flirting with her and why would Lord James Fitzroy ever think of flirting with *her*?

She cleared her throat and quickly changed the subject. "Um... so whose office is this?"

"It was traditionally the Steward's Office," said James. "But now it's just used as a general office by several members of the staff. The household accounts and other documents are kept in here, as well as our new brochures and marketing material for hosting events and tour groups."

Caitlyn looked thoughtfully around. She felt like something was wrong—something was off-balance— then she realised what it was. "There aren't any computers," she said in surprise. "I'm so used to offices nowadays having computers—"

"Yes, that's something I've been trying to change

since I returned to the Manor," said James. "My father was quite a technophobe and he didn't like computers or the internet or any kind of modern gadget. In fact, he made it a point of honour to ban computers at the Manor and stick to the 'old ways'. And I'm afraid that many of the older members of the staff—and villagers too—were quite in sympathy with him. I suppose people never like change, especially when you're older, and all this technology seems so alien." He made a rueful face. "And I confess, I probably haven't pushed things as hard as I could have. I knew that many of the older staff members and village residents were already anxious about me stepping into my father's shoes. I didn't want to rock the boat too much in the beginning and insist on changes which might cause resentment. So I've been taking things slowly. The younger members, like Lisa, my Events Coordinator, have been fine—in fact, she has her own laptop which she takes around with her—but the older members, like Mrs Brixton, were adamant that they didn't want any of the systems computerised. She was even suspicious of online banking and preferred to use cheques and visit the bank in person."

"Really?" Caitlyn said incredulously, wondering how anyone could still prefer depositing cheques in person to online banking.

"Yes," said James with a long-suffering smile. "And it makes the accounting a bit of a nightmare.

For example, the Garden Party has its own expense account and Mrs Brixton used to record all the information about expenses in handwritten entries in an old-fashioned ledger, which is really bulky to carry around—but she insisted on using it."

They were interrupted by the sound of soft footsteps outside the door of the office, which had swung shut. James leaned over and pulled the door open.

"Oh!" A middle-aged woman with stiff permed hair jumped as the door was pulled back. It was Winifred Harris, from the village committee.

"Mrs Harris," said James in surprise. "Can I help you?"

"Er..." The woman looked a bit furtive and fiddled with her handbag. There came the jingle of keys, then she pulled out a tissue and dabbed her forehead nonchalantly. "So hot today, isn't it?"

Caitlyn wondered suddenly if the nosy woman had been trying to eavesdrop on her and James's conversation.

"It is very pleasant," said James, looking a bit bewildered. "Is there something I can help you with?" he asked again.

"I was... er... wondering who is in charge of the Garden Party accounts, now that Mrs Brixton is dead," said Mrs Harris importantly. "There are... um... a few things I need to check."

Hah, thought Caitlyn. *A likely story.* It was so obviously a lame excuse for the woman's nosing around. She knew that Tillyhenge was constantly buzzing with speculation about her sudden arrival in the village, her stay at the chocolate shop, and her new friendship with the lord of Huntingdon Manor—she wouldn't put it past Winifred Harris to try and snoop around to get more juicy gossip.

"I'm afraid I haven't assigned a dedicated person to take over Mrs Brixton's role in that regard yet, Mrs Harris," said James. He indicated the antique writing desk behind them. Caitlyn noticed now that it had a slanted top with a hinge, which opened to reveal a compartment beneath—rather like a fancy school desk. "The account ledgers are all kept in there and I can spare a minute to go over things with you, if you like—"

"Oh, no, that's all right, Lord Fitzroy," said Mrs Harris hurriedly. "It's nothing important, really. And I can see that you're *very* busy with Miss Le Fey at the moment," she added with a meaningful look at Caitlyn, which made the latter flush. "I'll see you at the party tomorrow."

Backing away, she turned and quickly let herself out of the side door into the gardens. James frowned, looking slightly puzzled, then he shrugged and turned back to Caitlyn, saying, "At the rate we're going, I hope there *will* be a party tomorrow."

"Everything seemed to be going well when I arrived," Caitlyn commented. "It looks fantastic so far."

James sighed. "We got very behind schedule with

the preparations, actually, following the murder, and then the police investigation and questioning delayed things even further. But the staff have been amazing. Everyone has been working practically around the clock to get things ready for the Garden Party."

"Have the police made any progress with the investigation?" Caitlyn asked.

James shook his head. "No, and frankly I think Inspector Walsh is getting quite frustrated with the lack of developments. The investigation seems to have ground to a halt. Oh, they have several suspects—"

"Including me," said Caitlyn wryly.

James acknowledged that with a smile. "Yes, including yourself. But I don't think they have enough conclusive evidence to make a firm conviction yet. Inspector Walsh is a very careful, methodical man and I think he wants to wait until he has a solid case before he makes an arrest."

Caitlyn felt a guilty pang as she thought of the conversation she had had with Pomona in the car yesterday. The police ought to know about Matt O'Brien's shaky alibi. That might help them build a case against him... assuming that he *was* the murderer, of course, she hastily reminded herself. The problem was, if Matt *wasn't* the murderer, she knew that Pomona would never forgive her for reporting him to the police. She sighed inwardly and wished she knew what to do.

"Is something the matter?" James looked at her in concern.

Caitlyn looked up into his warm grey eyes. She was so tempted to tell him. There was something about James Fitzroy that always made her feel like she could trust him and tell him anything. But just as she opened her mouth to speak, an attractive young woman with blonde hair and an English-rose complexion popped her head into the office.

"James, could you come and check the—Oh, sorry." She smiled at Caitlyn. "I didn't mean to interrupt."

"Amy!" said Caitlyn in surprise. The last time she had seen Amy Matthews, the pretty widow had been under suspicion for the murder of her husband, Stan—who had been Lord Fitzroy's gamekeeper.

As if sensing her curiosity, Amy said, "James has been so kind! He offered me a position here at the Manor, to work as an assistant to Lisa, his Events Coordinator. I'd been despairing of ever finding work in the local area and this has been a godsend."

"Not at all," said James gallantly. "I'm sure Lisa would say that *you* are the godsend, Amy." He smiled warmly and Amy blushed.

Caitlyn felt a queer little tug at her heart as she looked at the two of them. They made such an attractive couple, with Amy so fair and James so dark, and both so tall and slim. She'd heard that since Stan's death, James had been very supportive to Amy, often visiting the widow in her cottage. Amy was still one of his tenants, of course, and Caitlyn knew that James felt a strong responsibility to all "his people"—but gossips in the village whispered and speculated over whether Lord Fitzroy's interest in the pretty widow went beyond that of a caring landlord.

Amy said, "I'm sorry to bother you, James, but Lisa wanted to check if you're happy with the final programme for tomorrow."

"I'll come right away." James gave Caitlyn an apologetic smile. "I'm afraid you'll have to excuse me—"

"Oh, don't worry about me," said Caitlyn quickly. "I'll... um... just go and find Pomona."

James scooped up the little kitten. "Come on, you little monkey. You're coming with me so that I can make sure you don't get up to more mischief."

Carrying the kitten in his arms, he left the room, with Amy and the mastiff following him.

CHAPTER THIRTEEN

Left on her own, Caitlyn decided to go back out the side door and re-enter the Manor from the front, so that she would have a better chance of getting her bearings. She didn't want to wander around lost again like her last visit. As she was entering the main foyer with its magnificent sweeping staircase and vaulted ceiling, she spied a dark figure skulking in the shadows farther down the main hall. She did a double take and rubbed her eyes, wondering if she was seeing things. No, there was no mistaking that tall, stooped figure or the dusty black suit that looked like a relic from the early nineteenth century. It was Viktor the old vampire.

What is he doing here? Caitlyn asked herself in exasperation. She hurried down the hall, hoping to catch him, but before she could reach him, he disappeared through a doorway and out of sight. Caitlyn arrived there a moment later to find that it was the entrance to the Library. She hadn't been in the Library at the Manor yet and now she felt that she was intruding slightly as she stepped into the hushed silence.

It was not a "cosy" kind of library but rather the type of sombre, formal room found in grand stately homes. The lighting was dim, despite large sash windows along one wall, and the ceilings soaring overhead reminded Caitlyn of cathedrals. The walls were filled floor to ceiling with dark mahogany bookcases, each displaying rows upon rows of neatly ordered books, and more bookcases were arranged in a series of rows running down the centre of the room.

The Library seemed to be empty and Caitlyn wandered slowly among the bookcases, marvelling at the number of volumes on display around her. She didn't think she had ever seen so many books in a private collection! The air was thick with the smell of old paper, dust, and leather, and dust motes danced in the shafts of sunlight that had managed to come through the windows and penetrate the library gloom.

A thud behind the next shelf reminded her of why she was here and she strained her ears to listen.

"Viktor? Is that you?" she whispered.

No sound.

Caitlyn frowned and crept forwards. She peered around the corner of the bookshelf, then jumped in fright as a plaintive voice said behind her:

"Have you seen my teeth?"

She whirled around. "Viktor! What are you doing here?" she hissed.

"Looking for my fangs, of course," he said huffily. "I thought they fell out in the greenhouse while I was having breakfast this morning. I was interrupted at the *most* inconvenient moment— really, how is one expected to get a decent meal when you have fools scurrying about like leprechauns hiding their pot of gold, I ask you—just as I was trying to decide between the figs and the nectarines... mind you, the grapes didn't look bad either... but I never—"

"This is the Library, not the greenhouse," said Caitlyn in exasperation. "Why are you looking for your fangs in here?"

"I was just coming to that," said Viktor irritably. "Impatience is a very unattractive trait in a young lady, you know."

"Viktor, you can't skulk around the Manor like this!" said Caitlyn, glancing nervously over her shoulder towards the door. "What if one of the staff sees you?"

He drew himself up indignantly. "I'll have you know, I am a vampire—I am well versed in the art of travelling through the shadows and remaining invisible. In fact, I have been sleeping in the Library for days and no one has seen me."

"You've been *what?*"

"Sleeping in the Library here. There's a nice warm corner up above the shelf of travel memoirs, and a handy little hook embedded in the cornice, for hanging upside down from. That's what I was trying to tell you earlier, if you'd had the courtesy to let me finish." He glowered at her. "I like to do my morning stretches here before I visit the greenhouse for breakfast. So it's possible I may have dropped my fangs then—"

"All right, all right, I'll help you look," said Caitlyn hastily. "Where do you think you might have dropped them? In which corner?"

She followed him to the back of the Library, where a corner shelf stood next to an armchair and a large glass cabinet. Viktor began complaining about having to shift the armchair to search in the corner properly but Caitlyn was no longer listening to him. Her gaze was riveted to the glass cabinet and she remembered James telling Inspector Walsh that the bloodstone ring had been kept in a glass cabinet in the Library.

She went up to the cabinet, pressing her nose against the glass pane to look at its contents. She recalled seeing the tourist group heading to the Library the day she had got lost in the house; it must have been part of the official tour of Huntingdon Manor and, as such, it made sense to have some items—things with historical or local interest—on display for visitors to see. This glass cabinet had obviously been put in so that those items could be displayed safely. It seemed to be filled with various Fitzroy family heirlooms and other curios, each with a little label and card giving more information about the item. There was a piece of parchment paper covered in spidery writing, for instance, which the accompanying card claimed was an original letter from Oliver Cromwell to one of the Fitzroy ancestors.

Caitlyn's interest, however, was focused on an empty spot within the cabinet where the red velvet lining was bare, except for a small photograph of a ring. The card next to the space read:

This bloodstone signet ring has been in the Fitzroy family for several generations and is believed to be imbued with powerful magic. Bloodstones are highly mystical stones, said to bring their owners riches and fame, and help overcome enemies in battle. In ancient times, they were treasured as amulets of protection, with an unrivalled ability to heal wounds, stop blood flow, draw out snake venom, and even cure tumours. Also known as heliotrope, bloodstones are usually dark green, with only small flecks of red—this ring contains one of the few rare stones that is almost completely red.

Caitlyn peered through the glass, squinting to see the photograph better. She hadn't seen a picture of the bloodstone ring yet and now, after reading all the romantic legends, she expected some kind of magnificent gem set in an intricately carved ring worthy of Gollum's lust... To her disappointment, however, the photograph showed a very ordinary-looking signet ring with a dull red oval stone; the kind of thing she wouldn't have given a second glance to if she had seen it in a junk shop. She began to wonder if James had been right and all the "mystical legends" stuff was just manufactured for the tourists' benefit.

A noise next to her reminded her of her companion and she turned to see Viktor looking under the armchair.

"Viktor," she called to him softly. "Viktor, do you know anything about this bloodstone ring? The one that's been stolen?"

"Eh?" He straightened and came closer, peering through the glass pane of the cabinet. He made an impatient noise as he read the card. "What a load of garlic!"

"Aren't the legends about the bloodstone true, then?"

Viktor sniffed disdainfully. "There *are* some bloodstones that are magical, but most of the ones being bandied about are just worthless trinkets. Of course, everyone likes to *think* that they have a magical bloodstone heirloom in their family." He leaned close to read the card again. "Really! From that account, you'd think that the Fitzroys owned the Ring of Sanguinum!"

"What's the Ring of Sanguinum?"

"Ah, well, if you are talking about magical bloodstones, *that* is the most valued one of all." Viktor wagged a finger at her. "It is a bloodstone ring which gives its bearer power over daemons, and other powerful dark magic. But it has been lost since antiquity and no one knows of its whereabouts now, if indeed it still exists."

"If it's been lost, then how do you know that the Fitzroy ring *isn't* the Ring of Sanguinum?"

"Because the bloodstone on the Ring of Sanguinum was engraved with the image of a bat," said Viktor. He peered through the cabinet again. "That is a photograph of the Fitzroy ring, is it not? I certainly do not see any engraving on the stone."

Caitlyn looked again at the photo and had to admit that Viktor was right. The Fitzroy bloodstone was smooth and opaque, its only special quality being its unusual dark red colour.

She sighed. "Well, I—" She broke off as she heard a sound from the other end of the Library. Carefully, she peeked around the edge of the bookcase which shielded this corner from view. She saw a young woman walking down the room, holding a feather duster and a rag. It was Amelia, Caitlyn realised with surprise. She thought James would have fired the maid, given that Amelia had been caught trying to steal from the house. She watched in dismay as the girl began running the duster along the shelves, working efficiently and swiftly down the rows.

She turned back to Viktor. "You've got to go!" she hissed. "One of the Fitzroys' maids has come in—it looks like she's cleaning the Library. She might see you! Maybe if you take your bat form, you can hide and then creep out without her noticing—"

"There is no need to do that," said Viktor loftily. "I told you that I am adept at moving through shadows. I can walk right past her without her seeing me. Watch this!"

Before she could stop him, he straightened his jacket, smoothed his hair over his balding pate, and sauntered out from behind the bookcase. Caitlyn heaved an exasperated sigh. Still, perhaps she was underestimating the old vampire—after all, he did say he had been sleeping in here for days and hadn't been discovered. Perhaps he really could "walk through shadows" and make himself invisible—

The air was rent suddenly by a piercing scream.

"Aaaaa-eeeeeeeek!"

CHAPTER FOURTEEN

Caitlyn scrambled out from behind the bookcase and nearly crashed into Amelia, who had run down to this end of the Library. She caught the maid by the shoulders and was rewarded with the girl thrashing around in a blind panic, screeching:

"Let me go! *Let me go!*"

"Amelia! It's me!" Caitlyn gave her a shake. "You're safe!"

The girl sagged in relief. "Oh! Oh my God, I thought... I thought I was..." She gasped for a breath, then she turned and pointed a shaking finger towards the other end of the library. "There was... there was a man—there! I saw him! With a white face an' white hands. Looked like someone risen from the dead, he did!"

"You must have made a mistake," said Caitlyn

quickly. "I've been in the Library for the past ten minutes and there's no one else in here."

"I saw him!" Amelia insisted. "He was there! This creepy old man in a black suit. He walked right past me!"

Cursing Viktor under her breath, Caitlyn pinned a bright smile on her face and said, "I think you probably imagined it. Maybe you saw a... um... a shadow and thought it was a man. These old rooms can have a creepy atmosphere sometimes and make you feel—"

"I didn't imagine nothin'!" said the girl, shaking her head vehemently. "I know what I saw! I have to go and tell Lord Fitzroy. He'll—"

"Uh... no, no, wait... er... don't you think you're over-reacting?" said Caitlyn desperately. She cast around for something to distract Amelia. Then she remembered the girl's position as a murder suspect. "Um... so have the police questioned you again?"

The maid's expression changed. "No... why should they?" she asked warily. "I told them—I had nothin' to do with Mrs Brixton's murder!"

"Oh, I wouldn't blame you even if you had," said Caitlyn smoothly. She lowered her voice. "I overheard what Mrs Brixton said to you, that day in her sitting room—she sounded like a horrible woman. I felt really sorry for you."

The girl's eyes widened and she stared at Caitlyn in astonishment for a moment, then a small smile tugged her lips. "Thanks," she said. "Yeah, she was a right cow, Edith Brixton. I mean, I'm sorry she's dead," she added hastily. "But everyone's been goin' around talkin' like it's such a tragedy an' nobody realised what a nasty piece of work she was!"

"Yes, I was shocked when I heard her threatening you," said Caitlyn, her voice full of sympathy.

The girl eyed her sideways. "I wasn't really stealin', you know. That's what I told the police. I was just helpin' someone out." Something in Caitlyn's expression made her add defensively, "For a small fee, of course. But you can't expect me to do all the work for nothin', can you? An' I needed the money. I have a sick mother, you see, an' she needs full-time nursing. I help to pay her medical bills."

Caitlyn felt a pang of pity, but then something—a glint in the girl's eyes—made her wonder how much of that sob story was true. She had a feeling that Amelia was the kind of girl who had a quick tongue and a knack for spinning a story so that she always came out looking good in any situation.

"What do you mean, 'helping someone out'?" she asked. "I thought the police said you received an anonymous note asking you to steal the ring. How would you have known whether you were helping somebody?"

"They explained in the note, see," said Amelia. "They said that the ring didn't belong to the Fitzroys. It was somethin' that the Fitzroys took from their ancestors an'... an' Lord Fitzroy would never miss it anyway! These rich, posh folk have so many things in their houses—he wouldn't even notice."

Caitlyn started to say that that still didn't make it right to steal, but bit her tongue on the retort. She didn't want to antagonise the girl. Instead, she said, "Do you have any idea who sent you the note?"

"The police keep askin' me that an' like I told them, I don't know," said Amelia sullenly.

"Was it handwritten?"

"Yeah, it was actually. In really dark ink—you know, like the kind of writin' from those old-fashioned fountain pens."

"Have you given the note to the police?" asked Caitlyn eagerly. "They'll probably have handwriting experts who can—"

"I did but the writin's gone."

Caitlyn stared at her. "What do you mean, 'the writing's gone'?"

The girl shrugged. "When I showed the note to them, it was blank. The writin' had disappeared." She shivered suddenly. "It was right creepy, if you ask me."

"Maybe the person used a trick ink—you know, the kind that fades with time or something like that," suggested Caitlyn lamely.

The maid didn't look convinced. "Maybe. The police couldn't figure it out either."

"Do you mean they have no way of tracing the

person who sent you the note?"

Amelia shook her head. "I think they're tryin' to trace the paper... see if they can find out where it comes from. But I don't know if that will tell them anythin'."

Caitlyn looked at the girl thoughtfully. She suddenly realised that there was no way of verifying Amelia's story. They only had her word that she had been sent an anonymous note but with the message on the note conveniently disappearing and no other lead, there was no proof that this anonymous person had ever existed.

What if it was just Amelia's quick tongue again, coming up with a clever story to cover up her own petty stealing? When the maid realised that she had been caught red-handed, she might have decided that it would make her look less guilty if she fobbed off the prime motivation behind the theft to this mysterious third party. It also made her look good too, in that she could say she had stolen the ring partly out of an altruistic desire to help another person regain what was rightfully theirs.

Caitlyn was beginning to realise why Inspector Walsh felt so frustrated with this investigation! There were too many suspicious circumstances and yet they all led nowhere and could all mean nothing!

"It's the curse of the bloodstone," said Amelia suddenly.

Caitlyn focused back on her. "I'm sorry?"

"Mrs Brixton's murder," said Amelia. "It's because she tried to prevent the bloodstone ring bein' returned to its rightful owner."

Caitlyn gave her a sceptical look. "I'm sure a lot of that is just superstitious non—"

"It's not!" the girl insisted. "Matt told me all about it. He's good with legends an' things like that, an' he said bloodstones have powerful magi—"

"Matt? Matt O'Brien?" Caitlyn said.

Amelia flushed slightly and Caitlyn wondered about the maid's feelings for the handsome gardener. After all, Amelia was a young, impressionable girl... and Matt O'Brien was exactly the kind of charming rogue that a lot of women fell for.

"How does Matt know so much about the bloodstone?" Caitlyn asked casually.

Amelia shrugged. "He's Irish. He says he was told lots of stories an' legends growin' up."

Maybe, thought Caitlyn. *But it still seems a strange coincidence.*

"Anyway, I'd better get on with the cleanin'." Amelia craned her neck to look back towards the other end of the Library, which was all quiet now. "Maybe you were right, maybe I did imagine it... although, I could have sworn I saw the old man..." Still muttering to herself, Amelia drifted back to the other side to continue her work.

Caitlyn looked surreptitiously around for Viktor but she didn't see him. He must have already made himself scarce. She left the library and walked back up the main hallway towards the foyer, deep in thought.

What if *Matt* was the person who had asked Amelia to steal the bloodstone? She could imagine that if Amelia had a crush on Matt, the maid wouldn't want the police to suspect him—so rather than say that Matt had asked her to steal the bloodstone ring, she had quickly made up the story about the anonymous note from the mysterious third party.

If that was true, then it meant that Matt could have murdered Mrs Brixton... He could have nipped out of the conservatory, done the deed, got the ring, then gone back to continue flirting with Pomona. He was just the kind of smooth, confident guy who could pull it off...

But what had he done with the ring? Caitlyn was sure that the police would have searched Matt's living quarters by now, so it couldn't be hidden there. Had he sold it off already? No, somehow she thought he would lie low for a while—wait until the hullaballoo from the murder had died down, before trying to get rid of it.

Which meant that the ring was still safely hidden somewhere... but where?

Caitlyn looked up as someone else came into the foyer. It was the other maid, Jenny. The girl was carrying an enormous flower display, made up of beautiful old-fashioned roses, peonies, freesias, and stocks, with trailing tendrils of jasmine.

"Wow, what gorgeous flowers," said Caitlyn. Then she laughed in delight as she saw the clusters of grapes tucked amongst the blooms. "Hey, there's even fruit in the arrangement! How creative."

"They taste fabulous too," said Jenny with a smile. "Matt O'Brien grows them in the greenhouse. He's a whizz with the fruits and veggies— Huntingdon could start supplying some of the local shops in the villages around here, if Lord Fitzroy was interested."

Caitlyn held the front door open for the maid, who thanked her and then carefully carried the flower display down the front steps and across the lawn to the tables set up for the Garden Party. As she watched Jenny go, Caitlyn thought about what the girl had just told her. Matt O'Brien again... Matt's name seemed to be coming up a lot, all of a sudden.

Then something else floated to the edge of her memory. Something about the greenhouse... She frowned, straining to remember. Someone else had been talking about the greenhouse recently... someone here at the Manor... but who was it?

Then it came to her in a rush: *Viktor!*

Yes, that was it. She remembered the old vampire grumbling in the library earlier about being interrupted while trying to have his breakfast. What was it he had said? Something like: *"...how is one expected to get a decent meal when you've got fools scurrying about like leprechauns hiding their pot of gold...?"*

At the time, she hadn't paid him much attention, but now she wondered at the old vampire's choice of words. Why had he mentioned leprechauns—a creature from *Irish* folk legend...? Caitlyn took a sharp intake of breath. Perhaps Viktor had been referring to Matt O'Brien! It would make sense of the Irish association. And perhaps he had observed Matt hiding something—which is why he made the comment about "scurrying about like leprechauns hiding their pot of gold". If Viktor had been spending a lot of time in the greenhouse in his bat form, enjoying the fruits being grown in there, he would have had ample opportunity to observe Matt's behaviour, without the gardener knowing that he was being watched.

She had to speak to Viktor again. But where could she find him? He could have been skulking anywhere in the Manor... Then the answer came to her: of course, the greenhouse! And in fact, that would kill two birds with one stone. She could ask Viktor about what he had seen—and check out the greenhouse herself. If Matt had got the ring, it would be the perfect hiding place. After all, with it being on Lord Fitzroy's estate, the greenhouse was less likely to draw suspicion than his own living quarters. And what better place to hide a stolen ring than a cluttered greenhouse filled with plants, vegetable patches, and flowers?

CHAPTER FIFTEEN

Caitlyn wandered casually across the front lawn and approached one of the garden boys who was busy pulling up weeds in a flowerbed.

"Hi..." She gave him a friendly smile. "Can you tell me where the greenhouse is, please?"

"Sure, you just go through the walled garden on the west side of the Manor and then take a right when you get to the gazebo. Follow the path down to the rear of the grounds. The greenhouse is on the south side."

"Thank you. Er... I don't suppose you know where Matt is?"

"He had to pop down to the village to get a few things."

"Ah, right... and is he going to be back soon?" she asked casually.

"Probably not for another half an hour. Old Palmer's in the potting shed, if you want anything— or maybe I can help you?"

"Oh no, it's nothing important," said Caitlyn quickly. She saw the garden boy grin and realised that he must have thought she was another of Matt's romantic conquests. She decided to let the assumption rest—at least that way she avoided any awkward questions about why she was interested in where Matt was.

Caitlyn followed the directions and soon found herself standing outside a beautiful traditional Victorian greenhouse. She looked furtively around: this side of the grounds was deserted at the moment, with all the staff busy on the front lawns, preparing for the party. That was good. Although she knew she wasn't really trespassing and that James would be more than happy for her to explore the Manor grounds, she still didn't want people to notice her snooping around.

She stepped inside and entered a humid space, filled with a riot of lush green. There were fruit trees—peaches and nectarines and figs and lemons—interspersed among beds of strawberries, cucumbers, and melons; a large vine of grapes climbing up one wall and arching overhead; glossy purple eggplants and cube-like red peppers showing off their bright colours, next to a bed of leafy lettuces and cabbages.

Caitlyn wandered slowly down one aisle, past

elegant olive trees and fragrant bay bushes growing in pots, and rows of staked tomato plants. It was all gorgeous and she would have loved to spend more time exploring the different plant varieties in here, but she felt a nagging sense of urgency. Matt could be back from the village any moment now and she didn't want to waste this opportunity to search the greenhouse.

But how was she going to find anything in this profusion of fruit and vegetables and greenery? She looked around helplessly. She didn't even know where to begin. The ring could have been hidden anywhere—buried in the soil under a melon somewhere, tucked into the side of a pot, hidden behind the leaves of a vine... not to mention stashed somewhere amongst the gardening equipment lining the corners of the greenhouse. She didn't see how she was ever going to find it without a guide of where to look.

Then she noticed something white on the other side of the greenhouse—it showed clearly amongst all the colourful greens. Curious, she went over to check it out. As she approached, she saw that it was a white plaster statue—a classic cherub standing in a coy pose, looking over a small pool. It was an ornamental water feature, Caitlyn realised; a jet of water shot out of the cherub's pursed lips and fell smoothly into the pool below, where goldfish darted between the water lily leaves.

Caitlyn circled the water feature speculatively.

She reached out and tapped the head of the cherub. It sounded hollow. She peered around the back of the statue, wondering if there would be any cavities or crevices for hiding things...

A hand gripped her shoulder.

"*Aaah!*" cried Caitlyn, stifling a scream as she whirled around.

A stooped old man in a dusty black suit stood in front of her.

"Viktor!" Caitlyn yelled. "You've got to stop scaring me like that!"

He looked so taken aback that Caitlyn felt bad for shouting at him. "I'm sorry," she said in a more normal voice. "I'm just a bit on edge right now..." She gave him a contrite smile. "I was hoping to see you here actually."

"I was just about to have a late morning meal— what I believe is called brunch, in this century," he said pompously. He smacked his sunken lips. "The nectarines are particularly nice at the moment. But what are *you* doing here, young lady?"

"I'm... uh... searching for something. Listen, Viktor—you know earlier in the Library you were talking about being disturbed while you're trying to eat in here—you mentioned something about leprechauns and pots of gold... Who were you talking about?"

"That handsome chap with the blue eyes," said Viktor irritably. "One of the gardeners, I believe. Very good with the fruits... I must say, the man knows his way around a nectarine tree—but he really should spend more of his time tending the fruit trees instead of messing about with his other crops."

"And... did you ever see him hide something?" she asked eagerly. "Like a ring, perhaps?"

"A ring?" Viktor looked at her like she was crazy. "Why would he hide a ring in here?"

"Because—oh, never mind, Viktor. Just tell me if you saw him hiding a ring?"

The old man frowned. "No, I never saw him hiding anything like a ring."

"Oh." Caitlyn was crestfallen. She had been so sure that she had been on the right track. "Well, then why did you say he was 'scurrying around like a leprechaun hiding a pot of gold'? You made it sound like he was doing something underhanded."

"He *is* always scurrying around," said Viktor. He pointed. "Over there, by the tomato plants. Furtive as a ferret."

Caitlyn followed the direction of his finger. "Do you mean... Matt is hiding something over there?" Not waiting for him to reply, she walked back to the far end of the greenhouse where a large patch of soil was devoted to rows of tomato plants. She peered amongst the tall staked green stems. She couldn't see anything unusual.

"Do you mean here?" she called.

There was no reply. She glanced over her shoulder. Viktor had disappeared. Probably gone off in search of his beloved nectarines. Sighing, she turned back to the tomatoes and stared at them again. She could just dismiss it—after all, Viktor's vision wasn't the best (to put it politely!) and he could have been wrong in what he saw. But something—some instinct—told her that Viktor was right to be suspicious. Matt O'Brien *was* hiding something here in the greenhouse. She just had to figure out what it was.

She gave another sigh of frustration. So much for being a witch! If only she knew how to work magic better, she could probably just conjure up a spell to show her what Matt had hidden here—

Wait.

She *did* know a spell.

Caitlyn thought excitedly back to the previous night when she and Evie were in the Widow Mags's bedroom, trying to see the photos in the enchanted album. Evie had made the hidden photos show themselves, hadn't she? Couldn't she, Caitlyn, do the same here?

Caitlyn closed her eyes, trying to remember the spell... what were the words? Something "*clandestine*"... no, "*clandestina*"... yes, "*manifesto clandestina*"... that was it!

She stepped closer to the tomato plants, held her hand out and concentrated hard, whispering, "*Manifesto clandestina!*"

There was a crackling sound and Caitlyn jumped as something sparked from her fingers. It felt a bit like the kind of static that jumped off your clothes sometimes. Then she forgot everything else as she suddenly realised that parts of the tomato patch were *glowing*.

She leaned closer to look. No, it wasn't the tomato plants that were glowing—it was individual smaller green plants amongst the tomatoes. If she had just been standing there, she would never have even have noticed them, and even now, as the glow around them faded, they were becoming harder to see again. They were well camouflaged amongst the feathery green tomato stalks and didn't have any particularly attractive distinguishing features—in fact, they looked like giant weeds, with leaves that had several palm-like fronds. As she leaned even closer to look, Caitlyn was suddenly aware of a sickly-sweet smell arising from the plants. She wrinkled her nose and drew back.

These strange green plants were obviously what Matt was hiding, carefully camouflaged here amongst the tomato plants—but what were they? Frowning, Caitlyn pulled her phone out of her pocket and quickly snapped a couple of shots of them. She was just pushing the phone back in her pocket when she heard a step behind her—Viktor back from his fruity "brunch", no doubt. She turned around eagerly.

"Look! I think I found—" She broke off, staring at the man in front of her.

"Hello, Caitlyn," said Matt O'Brien, his beautiful

blue eyes cold and suspicious. "What are you doing here?"

CHAPTER SIXTEEN

"Matt!" Caitlyn, faltered, taking an involuntary step back. She forced a breezy smile. "Hi! I... uh... just came to check out the greenhouse. I'd heard so much about the fruits and vegetables you were growing here..."

"Really?" He took a step towards her. "Didn't realise you were so interested in horticulture."

"Yes, um... well... I wouldn't say I'm a huge botanist or anything... haha..." Caitlyn laughed nervously. "But I'd been hearing everyone talk about the greenhouse and... um... I saw one of the flower arrangements for the Garden Party which included the most luscious-looking grapes..." She shifted farther back from him.

She was horribly aware again of how deserted this side of the Manor grounds was and how far away the rest of the staff were. Would anyone hear her if she screamed and called for help from inside the greenhouse? And even though the walls of the greenhouse were glass, the profusion of plants inside meant that it was hard for those on the outside to see in clearly.

"You were saying you found something just now..." Matt said in a silky voice. "What were you referring to?"

Caitlyn forced herself not to glance involuntarily at the tomato patch. "Oh... um... just... just the tomato patch. I love tomatoes. I... er... I suppose I'm pronouncing that wrong for England, aren't I? It's funny how I say some things the British way and some things the American way... I suppose it's because I had a British nanny so I grew up learning the British pronunciation of things and then we travelled around so much and hardly ever lived in the States, so I didn't really pick up much of an American accent... although I have to say, I've always preferred saying 'to-may-to', rather than 'to-mah-to', as you would say it... haha... Or I suppose... would the Irish say it any differently...?"

She was babbling now and she knew it, but she couldn't help herself. Matt was watching her with narrowed eyes and something in his expression chilled her.

He took another step forwards and made as if to grab her arm but a flurry of movement behind him made him jerk around.

A large fruit bat came flapping towards them, emitting a series of high-pitched squeaks that made Caitlyn wince and want to plug her ears. It hovered around Matt's head, dive-bombing him and spitting at him.

"Feck! It's that bloody bat again! GET OFF ME!" cried Matt angrily, trying to dodge the bits of nectarine pulp being spat in his face. He danced around, waving his arms, staggering down the aisle as he tried to chase the bat away.

Caitlyn used the opportunity to dart quickly past him and make for the greenhouse door. Once outside, she lost no time running back towards the front of the house. She could still hear Matt's angry cries fading away behind her and she smiled to herself. Good ol' Uncle Viktor to the rescue again. She had to admit that although she'd often scoffed at him when he proclaimed himself to be her "guardian protector", the old vampire really had saved her skin in several sticky situations and she was very grateful.

She arrived back at the front of the Manor, flushed and out of breath, and was delighted to see Pomona standing at the edge of the lawn, watching the preparations for the party.

"Pomie!" she hissed, running over and grabbing her cousin by the elbow. She dragged her around the other side of the house and found a secluded garden bench tucked behind a bush.

"What's the matter?" Pomona looked at her

157

curiously. "Why were you running?"

Caitlyn ignored her and pulled out her phone, scrolling quickly to a picture of the strange plants and shoving it under her cousin's nose.

"Look... do you have any idea what these plants are?"

Pomona peered at the screen, sliding her fingers across the surface to zoom in on the image. "It looks like... hey, it's a cannabis plant!"

"A cannabis plant? You mean, like marijuana? How do you know?"

Pomona laughed and rolled her eyes. "Everyone knows what a cannabis leaf looks like!"

"I don't," said Caitlyn.

Pomona gave her a dry look. "That's 'cos you spent your teenage years with your nose buried in books, instead of going out to parties. Trust me, I know what I'm talking about. Those are cannabis plants. That's, like, a nice little crop of marijuana that someone is growing there... Where did you find it?"

"In the greenhouse." Caitlyn watched her cousin closely. "The one that's looked after by Matt."

Pomona protested, "That doesn't mean that he—"

"It's him, Pomie. In fact, he found me in the greenhouse and I thought he was going to do something to me..." Caitlyn shuddered at the memory. "I managed to get away but he really scared me. That's why I was running."

Pomona still looked unwilling to accept Matt's

guilt. "Well... a lot of people probably grow a bit of marijuana... you know, as a recreational thing..."

"It's still a class B drug! You can get arrested for having it. And it's worse if you're found growing it because then you could be a supplier..." Caitlyn paused and thought for a moment, then said, "Remember the police saying that other staff had overheard Matt and Mrs Brixton having a fight? And he had threatened her to keep her mouth shut? I think it was about this. I thought Matt might have been involved in the theft of the bloodstone ring but I was wrong—that's something else. I don't know if Mrs Brixton was murdered for the ring... but she could have been murdered because of this! She must have found out that Matt was growing cannabis in the Manor greenhouse and she was trying to blackmail him to pay her, so that she wouldn't report him." Caitlyn paused again and added softly, "You have to agree that it gives him a very good motive for wanting Mrs Brixton dead..."

"Matt wouldn't do that," said Pomona, shaking her head vehemently. "Okay, so he might have been growing some pot—but that doesn't mean that he would commit murder!"

"He might if he felt that he was backed into a corner. He's a proud guy—he wouldn't be happy to be controlled by Mrs Brixton. And blackmail is never-ending. People feel trapped by it. They get desperate—"

"Not Matt," insisted Pomona stubbornly. "I know

him—he wouldn't murder anyone."

"We have to at least let the police know," said Caitlyn. "They can investigate and if Matt is really innocent—"

"NO!" cried Pomona. "No, you can't tell them! They're already prejudiced against Matt 'cos of his criminal record. They'll just jump on him immediately and stop looking anywhere else. He's, like, the perfect scapegoat. And that means that the real murderer will get away!" She grabbed Caitlyn's arm urgently. "You can't say anything—promise me! Please, Caitlyn," she begged.

Caitlyn stared at her cousin, torn over what to do. A part of her wanted to insist on telling the police. She didn't trust Matt O'Brien at all and, in spite of what Pomona had said, she was sure that the handsome Irishman was capable of committing a murder. But on the other hand, Pomona did have a point—what if Matt wasn't the murderer? It was true that just having a secret marijuana crop didn't automatically make him a killer. He might have simply threatened Mrs Brixton and left it at that.

And Caitlyn was also aware that there were still other suspects: Amelia, for instance, and the mystery of the anonymous note asking her to steal the bloodstone ring... The maid herself could have killed Mrs Brixton... or the writer of the note, if such a person really existed... After all, it was true that the ring was still missing and if Matt wasn't involved in its theft, then who was?

Caitlyn sighed. "All right, I... I won't say anything for *now*," she said, emphasising the last word. "But after the Garden Party is over tomorrow... well, I suppose I'll decide then."

Pomona looked as if she wanted to protest some more, but she could see that Caitlyn wasn't going to be persuaded further. She bit her lip, then nodded and said, "Thanks. Okay, that's fair, I guess."

"In the meantime—" Caitlyn broke off as she heard her name being called.

Both girls stood up from the bench and walked out of the secluded corner. They were surprised to see a uniformed constable standing on the other side of the garden.

"Miss Le Fey? Caitlyn Le Fey? Are you there?"

"I'm here," Caitlyn called, walking over to meet him, with Pomona at her heels.

"Please come with me, miss. The inspector would like to speak to you," he said formally.

Wondering what this was all about, Caitlyn followed the young constable around the side of the house and back out to the gravel driveway which swept around the front of the Manor. She saw Inspector Walsh standing at the edge of the front lawns, on the other side of the driveway. He had a companion—a short man in his sixties, wearing a brown tweed three-piece suit and old-fashioned spectacles perched on the end of his nose. They looked up as the girls approached, then the bespectacled man jumped forwards and jabbed a finger in Caitlyn's direction.

"That's her!" he cried excitedly. "That's the girl who brought me the stolen ring!"

CHAPTER SEVENTEEN

Caitlyn stared at the strange man, then looked at Inspector Walsh in confusion. The CID detective cleared his throat and beckoned the girls over to join them.

"We circulated the description of the stolen ring yesterday afternoon," he explained. "Mr Digweed here contacted us this morning. He says that a young lady brought a ring, which matched the description of the stolen bloodstone ring, into his antique jewellery store yesterday morning."

"Yes!" said the man, fairly dancing around in his excitement. "Yes, and I tell you—it's her! It's this girl here!" He pointed frantically at Caitlyn.

"Now, are you quite sure, sir?" asked Inspector Walsh. "It may be possible that—"

"Of course I'm sure!" cried Digweed indignantly.

"You can't miss that red hair." He thrust his nose in Caitlyn's face and scowled at her. "Thought you could fob off stolen property on me, did you? Thought you could trick me, eh?"

"I..." Caitlyn stared at him, dumbfounded. "I don't know what you're talking about! I've never met you before in my life."

"Don't try to wriggle out of it!" cried Digweed. "You came into my shop yesterday morning and showed me the stolen ring. You asked me to clean it—"

"Are you sure it couldn't have been another girl, sir?" asked Inspector Walsh again. "Perhaps you didn't see her clearly and she merely resembled Miss Le Fey superficially."

"Yeah, maybe you forgot what she looked like and are just jumping on Caitlyn 'cos she's got red hair," said Pomona.

Digweed glared at her. "My memory is crystal clear, thank you very much! I can even tell you what she was wearing: she had sunglasses and high heels and a one piece what-do-you-call-them things... a jumpsuit, like Jane Fonda in *Charlie's Angels*."

"Hang on, hang on!" cried Pomona. "Jane Fonda wasn't in *Charlie's Angels*."

Digweed jutted his chin out. "Of course she was! She was the blonde one."

Pomona rolled her eyes. "That was Farrah Fawcett!"

"No, no, it was Jane Fonda," insisted Digweed. "She had big bouffant blonde hair."

"I'm telling you it wasn't Jane Fonda in *Charlie's Angels*!" Pomona's voice was getting shrill with exasperation. "Boy, if you're mixing up Jane Fonda and Farrah Fawcett just 'cos they had the same hair, I don't think we can trust your identification of Caitlyn as the girl with the stolen ring either!"

Inspector Walsh was obviously coming to the same conclusion. Clearing his throat, he turned to Digweed and said: "We are grateful for your assistance, sir, but perhaps you would like to revise your statement—"

"What do you mean, revise my statement? I stand by what I saw," Digweed blustered. "Just because this *girl* here..." he shot a baleful look at Pomona, "...is trying to cast aspersions on me—"

"What's going on?" James Fitzroy came suddenly out of the front entrance of the Manor, followed by his English mastiff.

"Lord Fitzroy." Inspector Walsh inclined his head. "Allegedly, Miss Le Fey was seen at an antique jewellery store in Gloucester yesterday morning. According to Mr Digweed, who owns the store, she showed him the stolen ring and asked him to clean it."

"But that's impossible," said James. "Miss Le Fey was here having breakfast with me for most of yesterday morning. In fact, you saw her yourself, Inspector, and I can personally vouch for the fact that she did not leave Huntingdon Manor until nearly eleven o'clock." He looked at Digweed. "What time did you see your young lady?"

"Around ten o'clock," Digweed admitted reluctantly.

"Well, that could not possibly have been Miss Le Fey. You must have made a mistake."

"But—!" Digweed's face went red and he looked for a moment as if he would burst into another tirade. But James's cool authority obviously made him think twice. He gave Caitlyn a resentful look and said sullenly, "Well, she looks a lot like her."

"I don't suppose you have any CCTV cameras installed in the shop?" asked James.

"Of course not!" said Digweed, outraged. "I run a respectable, old-fashioned establishment, sir. I certainly don't have cameras spying on people!"

"You said the girl asked you to clean the ring," said Inspector Walsh. "Do you know why she did that?"

The little man drew himself up proudly. "Ah, that is because I specialise in cleaning and restoring antique rings. There is no other jeweller quite as experienced as me in the whole county—perhaps in the whole of England! Even the Queen herself once asked me to Buckingham Palace to seek my opinion on the cleaning of a ring in Her Majesty's collection."

"Yes, yes, I'm sure your skills are exemplary, Mr Digweed, but what I meant was, did she want the stolen ring cleaned for a particular reason?"

Digweed frowned. "In a way. It was slightly bizarre, to tell you the truth. She showed me the ring and told me that it was very old and needed a thorough clean. In particular, she said, the stone needed polishing."

"Why was that strange?" asked Inspector Walsh.

"Well, on first inspection, sir, it all looked fine to me. There didn't seem to be that much grime on the ring and the stone itself looked very clean. I even suggested to the girl that it probably didn't need cleaning and that additional polishing wouldn't increase the stone's lustre either. But she insisted and was prepared to pay for my time, so I agreed to do the job."

"When did she come back to collect the ring?"

"She asked me to have it ready by yesterday evening and said she would pay extra for the express service. She came to pick it up just as the shop was closing. She paid cash," he added, as if sensing the inspector's next question. "So I don't have any credit card records or similar."

"Did the ring need cleaning after all?" asked James.

Digweed turned back to him. "Yes, that is what was so strange. When I started to work on it, I found that, in fact, there *was* grime and dirt on the ring—at least, it was coming off on the cleaning cloths! But it didn't appear dirty when you just looked at it. And the bloodstone... ah, now that was

167

the strangest part of all. As I polished it, an engraving on the surface of the stone seemed to appear."

"An enchanted ring!" Pomona whispered excitedly in Caitlyn's ear.

"Are you sure?" James looked disbelieving. "Engravings are cut into the surface of a stone. They can't just appear like that."

"This one did," Digweed insisted. "I was quite flabbergasted when I noticed it."

"What was the engraving?" Pomona asked eagerly

Digweed screwed his eyes up. "I couldn't say with certainty. It looked like a pair of wings—"

"Butterfly wings?"

"No."

"Angel wings?"

"No, no... more like... bat wings."

"I don't suppose you took a photograph of the engraving?" asked the inspector hopefully.

"No, of course not," said the jeweller, affronted again. "I respect people's privacy and I would never make a visual record of their jewellery without their permission!" He calmed down slightly. "In any case, I had no idea that it was a stolen item. I didn't see the police circular until this morning—and I called the station as soon as I realised!"

"Yes, yes, very indebted to you, sir," muttered Inspector Walsh. "Thank you, Mr Digweed—you have been more than helpful. One of the constables will go over your statement and drive you back to your store."

The little man bustled off with a uniformed constable, leaving the rest of them standing on the front lawns.

"It wasn't me," Caitlyn spoke. "I really don't know who he saw but I can promise you, Inspector, that it wasn't me. I never saw that man before today!"

Inspector Walsh gave her a thoughtful look. "Hmm... yes, well..."

"Inspector, surely you have to accept that Caitlyn—I mean, Miss Le Fey, has a rock-solid alibi this time?" asked James impatiently.

The inspector held his hand up placatingly. "Yes, yes, I am not questioning her alibi, especially since I saw her myself yesterday morning. I was thinking something else: red hair isn't that common but it is a very recognisable trait. Either we have to believe that by a very great coincidence, the thief who murdered Mrs Brixton and stole the ring also had red hair or..."

"Or they wore a red wig on purpose!" said Pomona.

The inspector nodded approvingly. "Yes, that is the other possibility that crossed my mind."

"But why?" asked Caitlyn. "Why would anybody want to impersonate me?"

"To throw suspicion your way and distract the police," said James. "Someone who knew that you were one of the suspects and thought that a red wig would be an easy way to muddy the waters."

Caitlyn didn't know what to say. To her relief, the inspector seemed to be fed-up with the whole thing and keen to return to his other investigations. After promising to keep James updated on any further developments, he took his leave.

It was only as his car drove down the driveway and out of sight that Caitlyn remembered the dilemma with Matt O'Brien. She sighed. Well, it was too late now. And she had promised Pomona not to say anything for the time being, she reminded herself. She would simply have to wait until after the Garden Party and make up her mind then.

James excused himself to return to his study, leaving the two girls alone on the front lawns.

"Are you going back to the village now?" Pomona asked her.

"Yeah, I was planning to—why?"

"Have you decided what you're wearing to the Garden Party?"

"What I'm wearing?" Caitlyn looked at her cousin blankly.

"Yes, your outfit for the party. Omigod, Caitlyn— don't tell me you haven't thought about it?"

"No," Caitlyn confessed. "There's been too much going on. Why—have you decided what to wear?"

"Of course! I thought about it the first time James mentioned the party to me. Luckily, I have a couple of little numbers in my overnight case that I keep in the car," said Pomona with a wink.

Caitlyn hid a smile. She was sure that Pomona's "overnight case" probably had a bigger range of fashion items than most people's entire summer wardrobes.

"Well, I didn't really bring anything smart with me to the Cotswolds," said Caitlyn. "It's mostly just jeans and T-shirts. Hey, it was supposed to be a vacation in the countryside—I wasn't expecting to have to dress up," she said defensively as she saw Pomona's look of derision.

"Well, you'll just have to borrow one of my dresses," said Pomona. "You can't turn up at the Manor tomorrow dressed in jeans and a T-shirt! This is, like, an English summer garden party, Caitlyn, and you know how proper British events always are. Everyone will be looking their best. It would be rude and disrespectful to James if you didn't follow the etiquette."

"Okay," said Caitlyn hesitantly. "But we're not really the same size, Pomie—"

"We're similar enough," said Pomona. "C'mon! Come up to my room and try on some of the things I've got."

Caitlyn followed her cousin back into the Manor. Pomona's room was similar to the elegant suite that she had stayed in two nights before and Caitlyn felt a slight pang of envy towards her cousin for getting to stay in such luxurious splendour. The place was a mess, though, with shoes kicked off everywhere and colourful clothes strewn all over the bed.

"Here... these should fit you..." said Pomona, dragging a couple of dresses out of the open case next to the bed. "I think the yellow would go fantastic with your red hair!"

Caitlyn surveyed the offerings doubtfully. She and Pomona had very different tastes. Her cousin was like a bird of paradise, loving anything bright and colourful—and the more sequins, the better! Caitlyn preferred her wardrobe in more muted tones of aubergine, olive, pale mauve, dove grey... and usually in soft natural fabrics like cotton and cashmere. She held up one of Pomona's dresses and regarded it warily. It was made of clinging Lycra and was covered in a geometric pattern of red and green.

"Try it on!" Pomona urged.

Caitlyn did as she was bid, then stared in horror at her reflection in the mirror. "I look like a sausage in Christmas gift wrap!" she cried.

"Oh, pul-lease!" said Pomona, grinning. "It looks great on you! Look how it shows off your curves."

"It's not showing off my curves—it's making me look fat! I want to hide my hips, not shine a spotlight on them!"

"Okay, okay—try this one then," said Pomona, handing her another dress, this time in an alarming shade of fuchsia.

Caitlyn tried on dress after dress and cringed a little bit more every time she looked in the mirror. Finally, she stood exhausted in the last dress that Pomona had handed her.

"You're so fussy!" Pomona said irritably. She mimicked Caitlyn's voice: "'Not too tight! Not too colourful! Not too short! Not too skimpy!' Seriously, Caitlyn, you've gotta loosen up a bit when it comes to your wardrobe. This is *fashion*, honey—it's supposed to be attention-grabbing. Anyway, you can't say no to this one—it ticks every box you were complaining about."

Caitlyn looked at her reflection. Well, at least the dress wasn't stretched tight across her thighs and hips... and the colour was okay: a sort of turquoise—still on the bright side but at least it was plain, with no patterns. And it was made of silk, which skimmed more than it clung. The neckline still plunged far lower than Caitlyn was comfortable with—she adjusted it again, trying to hitch it up a bit higher so as not to show so much of her cleavage—but compared to some of the other dresses, it was practically prudish.

In any case, Pomona was right. She didn't have anything else suitable of her own and she had to wear a decent dress to the party tomorrow.

"All right," she said with a resigned sigh, hoping that she wouldn't regret it. "I'll wear this one."

CHAPTER EIGHTEEN

Caitlyn drove slowly back to Tillyhenge, her thoughts divided between the murder investigation and the dress she would have to wear to the Garden Party tomorrow. Both subjects made her uneasy and she kept wondering if she had made the right decision in both cases.

As she was locking her car, she heard her name being called and looked up in surprise to see Angela Skinner approaching her across the village green. She hadn't seen the other woman since the day they'd met at the stone circle—the day Mrs Brixton was murdered, Caitlyn reminded herself. Angela was walking towards her now with a friendly smile. It was so unexpected that Caitlyn almost did a double take.

"Hello, Caitlyn! How are you?"

"I... I'm fine," stammered Caitlyn.

"I came to apologise," said Angela, to Caitlyn's even greater astonishment. "About your alibi," she added. "When Inspector Walsh questioned me, it completely slipped my mind that we'd met by the stone circle... how silly of me!" She gave a tinkle of laughter. "It didn't cause too much trouble for you, did it? I hope you'll forgive me?"

Caitlyn shifted uncomfortably as the other woman looked at her with wide, innocent eyes. "Er... yeah, sure. It's no big deal."

Angela beamed. "I'm so glad! You know, I've been thinking—we got off on the wrong foot, as they say, and I'd really like to wipe the slate clean and start again. So as a gesture of goodwill, I wanted to tell you that I'd be happy to give you a discount at my boutique."

"Your boutique?"

"Oh, didn't you know? I own a little dress boutique." Angela gave a coy smile. "It's one of the top fashion destinations in this area of the Cotswolds; I pride myself on stocking key pieces from the latest catwalk shows. In fact, I've got some fabulous summer dresses at the moment—have you got a dress to wear to the Fitzroy Summer Garden Party?"

"Er... sort of," mumbled Caitlyn.

"Oh, you must come and have a look at my range!" cried Angela. "There's one dress which would be just *perfect* with your colouring! Come on,

I must show you..." She grabbed Caitlyn's arm and began dragging her across the village green.

Caitlyn hesitated. Her distrust of Angela was still strong but, on the other hand, she felt churlish for not responding to this offer of an olive branch. If Angela was keen to make amends, then she should be generous enough to match the other woman's efforts.

So she let herself be led across the village green and down the main street of Tillyhenge, which hosted most of the shops in the village. They entered a boutique about halfway down and, as Caitlyn stepped inside, she had to admit to herself that whatever else she might think of Angela, the woman had great taste. The dresses on the mannequins were glamorous, elegant affairs, reeking of Paris and Rome, rather than frumpy middle England, and in the most beautiful combination of colours. She couldn't help herself from reaching out to touch the sleeve of a floral sundress on a mannequin by the door.

"That one is lovely, isn't it?" commented Angela. "It's been one of my bestsellers this season. But not on you, darling—that yellow would clash with your hair. *This* dress, however, is absolutely made for you!"

She led the way to the back of the shop and pulled a dress off one of the racks. Caitlyn took a sharp breath. It was gorgeous. Made of a soft, floaty chiffon fabric, in a kaleidoscope of shimmering greens, from jade to aqua, emerald to mint, the dress had dainty straps attached to a fitted bodice, then skimmed the waist and fell in graceful folds to the ankles. It looked like something a sea goddess would wear as she rose out of the ocean.

"You've got to try it on!" said Angela enthusiastically.

A few minutes later, Caitlyn stood surveying herself in the cramped changing room. The dress looked even more gorgeous on her than on the hanger, which was a feat in itself. Again, she had to grudgingly admit that Angela had a great eye for colour and style—the other woman had been right that the mix of soft greens went perfectly with Caitlyn's colouring, bringing out the glossy red of her hair and making her skin look creamier and her hazel eyes more startling. For the first time in her life, Caitlyn felt glamorous and beautiful. She wondered suddenly what James would think of her in this dress...

"How does it look? Do come out and show me!" called Angela from outside the changing room door.

Caitlyn stepped out almost shyly and stood in front of the other woman.

Angela gasped. "You look *fabulous*, darling!" She grabbed Caitlyn by the shoulders and turned her around to face the full-length mirror on the wall.

Caitlyn pivoted and turned to see the side view, then she frowned slightly. She realised that because of her pear-shaped figure, although the dress fitted perfectly on top, it was slightly too tight around her bottom half. As she moved, the bulges on her hips and belly were visible, not to mention the wobble of her thighs, and she winced as she watched her reflection.

"It's beautiful... but it's... a bit too tight around here, isn't it?" she said, gesturing awkwardly to her hips and bottom.

"Oh, that's easy to fix," said Angela, grabbing a pin cushion and kneeling down next to Caitlyn. "I just need to let the seams out a little bit, give you a bit more room..." She pinned a few spots on the dress. "Don't worry, I can do that in a jiffy this evening. I'll adjust it and have the dress sent to you at the chocolate shop tomorrow morning. You'll have it in time to wear to the party."

"Wow... thanks. That's really kind of you," said Caitlyn, feeling ashamed now of her earlier suspicious attitude.

Angela gave Caitlyn a conspiratorial smile. "Well, us pear-shaped girls have to stick together, don't we?"

Caitlyn wondered what Angela could mean since she was as thin as a rake and looked more like a string bean than a pear. But she kept her thoughts to herself and simply thanked the other woman again. She paid for the dress and finally left the boutique with a slightly surreal feeling. She had certainly never imagined that she would spend a "girlie afternoon" shopping with Angela Skinner!

She walked back to the chocolate shop in a happy daze, thinking excitedly about the rest of her outfit. She had a pair of strappy sandals which she could wear with the dress. They weren't very glamorous but hopefully, since the dress was long, people wouldn't notice her feet much anyway. And her hair? Maybe she could attempt to put it up in an elegant chignon, to accentuate the line of her neck...

Caitlyn came out of her daydreaming as she approached the chocolate shop and noticed that there was a familiar figure standing outside the window. It was Molly, the little girl with the pigtails. She was staring wistfully through the glass at the chocolates in the window display.

"Hi, Molly," said Caitlyn softly as she came up behind the girl.

The six-year-old whirled around in alarm, then relaxed slightly as she recognised Caitlyn. "Hullo..." she said shyly.

"Do you like chocolates?" Caitlyn asked, glancing at the glass pane. The Widow Mags had changed some things in the window display, adding several new items she had created for the Garden Party.

The little girl smiled, showing a gap in her front teeth, and nodded.

"Me too," said Caitlyn, returning the girl's smile. "What's your favourite kind?"

Molly shrugged shyly, looking down and fiddling with her dress.

Caitlyn tried again. "What about the things in the window—which one do you think would be your favourite?"

The girl looked up and pointed eagerly through the pane. "Those!"

Caitlyn saw that she was pointing to a container filled with milk chocolate lollipops in the shape of smiley faces. They were a new design that the Widow Mags had just started making.

"Those look cute, don't they? Would you like to try one?"

Molly looked uncertain. "Mummy said I'm not supposed to..."

"Oh." Caitlyn hesitated. She didn't want to go against the girl's mother's rules. "Is it because you're not supposed to eat sweets before dinner or something like that?"

Molly shook her head. "No, she says I can eat sweets from the other shop but not from this one... because the witch lives here!" She threw a scared look through the open doorway of the shop.

Caitlyn felt a flash of irritation at the girl's mother but she didn't let it show on her face. Instead, she crouched down next to the girl and gave her a reassuring smile. "Molly, I promise you there's nothing to fear from the old lady who owns the shop."

"She's a witch though, isn't she?" asked Molly.

"Um..." Caitlyn wondered if this was one of the times when it was okay to tell a white lie. "Well, she's certainly got a special magic with chocolates."

"You mean, she's a chocolate witch?"

Caitlyn suppressed a laugh. "Yeah, I suppose you could say that."

Molly gave Caitlyn a tentative smile and said, "In stories, sometimes there's a good witch and a bad witch."

Caitlyn nodded. "Oh, the Widow Mags is definitely a good witch! After all, how could any witch who makes such delicious chocolates be bad, right?"

The little girl giggled.

On an impulse, Caitlyn ducked into the store and reached into the window display, lifting out one of the chocolate smiley face lollipops. She came back out and offered it to the girl. "Here you go. Try it and see what you think."

The little girl beamed, but just as she was about to reach for the lollipop stick, a sharp voice interrupted them.

"Molly Jenkins! You'd better not be thinking of taking that!"

The little girl gasped and jerked around. Marching up to them was a middle-aged woman with a stiff perm. It was Winifred Harris, from the village committee. She frowned at Molly.

"What are you doing here? Your mummy is looking for you."

The little girl gave her a fearful look, then turned and ran off down the lane.

Winifred Harris glared at Caitlyn. "What do you think you're doing? How dare you corrupt the children of this village?"

"It's only chocolates," said Caitlyn, taken aback. The way the woman was acting, you would have thought that she had been offering Molly drugs!

Mrs Harris narrowed her eyes. "These aren't normal chocolates. They are bewitched—full of dark magic! It's bad enough that we have to have them at the Garden Party, without you peddling them in the street too!"

She stalked into the shop and Caitlyn hurried after her. Mrs Harris marched over and faced the Widow Mags and Bertha across the counter. The two witches paused in their conversation and looked at her in surprise.

"I don't know how you did it," she said, jabbing a finger at the Widow Mags. "You must have bewitched Lord Fitzroy too—cast some evil spell on him, to convince him to include your abominable chocolates in the Garden Party menu!"

Bertha gasped in outrage. "That's a lie! My mother would never use dark magic that way, and anyway, she wouldn't need to! Her chocolates are delicious and *that's* the reason Lord Fitzroy asked for them to be included on the menu."

"Don't you dare call me a liar!" cried Mrs Harris shrilly, her face getting red. Her hands clenched spasmodically. "I know evil when I see it! And I won't have it, do you hear me?"

"It's not your party, woman," growled the Widow Mags. "If Lord Fitzroy is happy to have my chocolates there, it is really none of your business."

Mrs Harris's face went purple and she looked as if she would burst a vessel. "YOU... YOU—!" She grabbed a glass jar of home-made chocolate sauce from the counter and raised it threateningly at the Widow Mags.

"Whoa...!" said Caitlyn, grabbing her arm. Good grief, the woman looked like she had serious anger management issues. Caitlyn almost felt sorry for her. Maybe if Winifred Harris didn't go around buttoned up so tight and bristling with respectability, she wouldn't be so cranky.

Mrs Harris calmed down slightly and shook Caitlyn's hand off her arm. She thumped the jar back down on the counter and said furiously:

"I might not be able to stop them being served but I'm going to make sure that nobody touches your filthy chocolates!"

She stormed out of the shop. There was an awkward silence after she left, then Bertha said brightly:

"So... what have you been up to, Caitlyn? I haven't seen you all day."

"I've been over at the Manor most of the day... and I've been shopping," said Caitlyn with a grin. "Getting my dress for the Garden Party tomorrow."

"Ohhh, Evie's very excited about that. Especially as Pomona has promised to come over tomorrow morning and show her the proper way to use mascara." Bertha chuckled. She adjusted her kaftan around her shoulders and said, almost girlishly, "I've got a new kaftan too, especially for the party—I thought I'd get one in a new shade."

"Oh? What colour?" asked Caitlyn with a smile.

"Purple!" Bertha beamed.

"Er... right." Caitlyn looked at the voluminous purple kaftan that Bertha was wearing at the moment. Every item of clothing she had ever seen the older woman wear had always been purple.

"Well, I'll come over tomorrow morning to help with the chocolates," said Bertha. "See you then!"

Left alone with the Widow Mags, Caitlyn fidgeted nervously and agonised over what to do. She hadn't forgotten her adventure with Evie last night and that picture in the photo album was still on her mind. She had meant to find a chance to ask the Widow Mags about the photograph this morning, but somehow things had got side-tracked with the murder investigation. Now, however—as she helped the Widow Mags shut up the shop and retire to the kitchen to rustle up something for dinner—she thought about mustering up the courage to ask about the photo.

The problem was, there was no way she could mention the picture without also admitting that she and Evie had been trespassing in the Widow Mags's bedroom and snooping through her things. They had even used a spell to reveal what the old witch had wanted to keep hidden. Caitlyn cringed at the thought of confessing their prying to the old woman. The Widow Mags would be furious and, to tell the truth, Caitlyn was a bit scared of her. She'd seen the old witch in action and she didn't want to end up with chocolate warts all over her body—or worse.

Besides, it wasn't just that—Caitlyn also felt guilty and ashamed of what she and Evie had done. It had been wrong of them to go through the Widow Mags's private belongings and there was no excuse for their behaviour.

Sighing, Caitlyn decided to follow the example of the Matt O'Brien dilemma and put things off until after the Garden Party.

CHAPTER NINETEEN

Caitlyn had planned to wake early the next day but she must have been more tired than she realised because, when she finally opened her eyes and looked blearily around, she was horrified to see that the clock on her bedside table showed that it was well past nine-thirty. Throwing on some clothes, she ran downstairs to find the Widow Mags already busy in the kitchen.

"Oh! You should have woken me!" she cried, eyeing the activity around her. "I was going to help you—"

"You needed the rest," said the old woman calmly. "Stop fussing, girl! The party doesn't start until 2 p.m. There is plenty of time. Go back upstairs—I don't want to see you back down here until you're showered and dressed."

Meekly, Caitlyn did as she was told, thinking to herself that the Widow Mags was acting like a bossy grandmother already! She followed the old woman's advice, though, and took her time washing her hair and drying it as thoroughly as she could with a towel, before dressing and going back downstairs.

"A package arrived for you." The Widow Mags pointed to a soft parcel, wrapped in brown paper and string, sitting on the kitchen counter.

"Oh, that must be my dress!" said Caitlyn in delight.

So Angela had kept her promise. Caitlyn was ashamed again of doubting the other woman's good intentions. Picking up the parcel, she held it close to her chest, feeling a little thrill of excitement. Dreamily, she wondered what James Fitzroy would think when he saw her—would he be surprised? Would he think she looked beau—

"Are you going to help me or are you going to stand there mooning about?"

Caitlyn started and blushed as she met the Widow Mags's sarcastic eye. Quickly, she laid the parcel back down, donned an apron, and approached the wooden table. The rest of the morning passed in a blur and Caitlyn was surprised when she finally looked up at the clock on the kitchen wall and saw that it was nearly one o'clock. James had thoughtfully sent some of his staff over to pick up all the chocolate fudge, truffles, bonbons, and other decadent treats and transport them over to the Manor. They had just left in the Range Rover and were returning soon for the final item: the chocolate fudge cake.

Well, "cake" was a bit of an understatement. It wasn't a cake—it was a chocolate masterpiece: four tiers of moist dark chocolate sponge, filled with milk chocolate buttercream and covered with rich chocolate fudge frosting, accompanied by dainty chocolate curls and shavings. And arranged around each tier of the cake were clusters of lush strawberries and raspberries, their jewel-red colours glowing against the deep brown.

The Widow Mags beckoned to Caitlyn and pointed to the tray next to the cake. "Those are the final touch. You can put them on the cake."

Caitlyn reached towards the tray, which held dozens of delicate chocolate filigree butterflies, just like the one she had made two days ago, and carefully picked one up with her thumb and forefinger. She reached up and placed it next to a juicy strawberry on the top tier, then stood back to admire the effect. Humming to herself, she continued adding chocolate butterflies to the rest of the cake, until all four tiers were randomly covered in dainty wings. She stepped back at last to see the result and sighed happily.

Now it really is *a masterpiece*, she thought, smiling. In fact, the cake looked almost too magnificent to eat.

"Are you sure they'll be okay transporting the

cake?" she asked the Widow Mags in concern. She winced as she imagined the men dropping the cake or even knocking it by mistake and damaging some of the decorations.

"This is why we add one more thing..." The Widow Mags pointed to a small bowl filled with snowy white powder. "Vanilla-scented icing sugar," she explained at Caitlyn's questioning look. "And mixed in with it, a little bit of... let's call it fairy dust, shall we?" The old woman grinned.

As Caitlyn watched, the Widow Mags scooped up a bit of the powdered sugar and placed it in the palm of her hand. Then, holding her flattened palm up to her lips, she blew gently towards the cake. The sugar billowed outwards in a white cloud, covering the surface of the cake in a soft white mist which sparkled with magic for a moment, then faded to look like an ordinary dusting of icing sugar.

The Widow Mags nodded with satisfaction. "There. I have put a charm on the cake now and it will be protected from damage. Don't worry, it will fade in a few hours... otherwise no one will be able to cut it!" She chuckled. Then she looked at Caitlyn and said, "Shouldn't you be getting ready, young lady?"

"Oh my goodness, yes!" cried Caitlyn, springing up and untying her apron. She glanced at the clock again. She had barely forty-five minutes to get dressed. Thank goodness she had washed her hair that morning!

She grabbed the parcel from the counter and hurried eagerly upstairs. Tearing the brown paper open, she sighed with pleasure as she looked at the dress again. It was just as beautiful as she remembered it. Quickly, she unzipped the back and stepped into it, then pulled the fabric gently upwards. It jammed around her hips. She looked down in surprise. Gently, she wriggled and tugged, trying to slide the dress further up her body. Surely it hadn't been this difficult to get it on at Angela's shop yesterday?

Maybe I've put on weight, thought Caitlyn guiltily. She wasn't sure how one day could have made so much difference but there were things like bloating, right? And if she was being perfectly honest, she had indulged in quite a lot of chocolates lately. Maybe it was all catching up with her now...

She sucked her stomach in and pulled and heaved again, managing to tug the dress up a few more inches—but now she was having trouble breathing and the dress had jammed again, bunching horribly around her hips. Caitlyn gasped for a breath, feeling light-headed, and looked down in despair. What was going on? Why was the dress so tight all of a sudden? She gave the dress another tug and heard the sound of fabric ripping.

Oh no!

Quickly, she peeled the dress off again and stepped out of the shimmering green folds. She held it up in front of her and stared at it in bewilderment. Then a dark suspicion entered her mind. Could it be...? No, that seemed too mean and small-minded. But now that the idea was in her head, it wouldn't go away.

Turning the dress inside out, she held it up to the light and examined the seams at the side. Her heart sank as she saw what she had suspected. Someone *had* gone through and re-stitched the seams, but instead of altering them so that it was looser around her hips, the dress had been *taken in* and was now smaller and tighter. No wonder she had struggled to get it on!

Caitlyn felt a flash of anger. It was Angela! Angela must have done this on purpose. She had pretended to be nice and helpful with that offer to let the dress out—and instead, she had stitched it up so that Caitlyn could barely get into it! Even if she did manage to eventually squeeze into it, the dress would be so horribly tight that it would show every ugly lump and bulge.

I'd been right to be suspicious of Angela Skinner's sudden friendliness, Caitlyn thought bitterly. She might have known that there would be an ulterior motive. Angela had concocted a very elaborate plan to find a way to get back at her. How the other woman must have laughed to herself yesterday when she had lulled Caitlyn into a false sense of security! And how she must have been enjoying the thought of humiliating Caitlyn at the party now.

Caitlyn sat down on the bed, clutching the dress

and feeling a sense of panic. What was she going to do now? It was nearly two o'clock and there was no time to undo the seams and re-stitch them in time for the party—and anyway, she had no dress-making skills. She could go back to wearing Pomona's dress, she supposed, although the thought made her heart sink. She had been so looking forward to wearing her new dress and feeling beautiful in it...

A knock at her bedroom door interrupted her dark thoughts. "Caitlyn?" came Bertha's voice. "We ought to go now. Are you ready, dear?"

"Er... No... not quite..." said Caitlyn breathlessly, springing up from the bed and looking frantically around.

"Caitlyn, is everything all right?" Bertha opened the door slightly and peeked in. Her expression changed to one of concern as she saw Caitlyn's face. "What's the matter?"

Caitlyn had been too embarrassed to admit her predicament but now, seeing Bertha's kind face and motherly manner, she suddenly wanted a shoulder to cry on.

"It's my dress... it's too small and I can't get into it!" she cried.

Bertha came into the room, a vision of purple in a lilac-and-lavender kaftan, and said, frowning: "Didn't you try it in the shop, dear?"

"Yes, I did!" said Caitlyn. "It fit fine up top but it was just a bit tight here..." She indicated her hips, embarrassed. "I'm wider in my bottom half..."

Bertha waved dismissively. "A womanly figure is nothing to be ashamed of."

"Yes, well, Angela said she would help me—she promised to alter the seams of the dress and let it out a bit, loosen it up... But I tried it just now and it looks like she's actually stitched it tighter!"

Bertha narrowed her eyes. "You mean, Angela did that on purpose?"

Caitlyn shrugged. "I don't know. I can't prove it but... I wouldn't be surprised. I thought it was a bit weird that she was so friendly to me yesterday, especially given how she snubbed me at the stone circle the other day. I think she's still mad at me and this was an elaborate trick to put me in a difficult situation, maybe humiliate me too."

"Hmm..." Bertha picked up the dress and examined it, then she brightened and looked at Caitlyn. "I know! All you need is some control shapewear and then you should be fine."

"There's no control shapewear that would make me fit into that dress," protested Caitlyn. "It's literally a whole size too small now."

"Ah, well, there is control shapewear... and *control shapewear*," said Bertha with a knowing smile. She gave Caitlyn a wink. "Don't worry, Cinderella—you *shall* go to the ball. Come downstairs with me and bring the dress with you. The shop is shut now so no one can see you."

Mystified, Caitlyn followed the older woman

downstairs to the kitchen, clutching the dress to her chest and feeling self-conscious dressed only in her underwear. They found the Widow Mags waiting at the table and Bertha quickly explained Caitlyn's predicament.

"Hmm..." The Widow Mags walked around Caitlyn, surveying her body with a critical eye. "Yes... yes..." She raised both hands suddenly. "Stand still, girl, and don't fidget."

Caitlyn gulped and held her breath. The Widow Mags waved one hand and, as Caitlyn watched in amazement, a wave of smooth, melted chocolate rose suddenly out of the big cauldron and glided slowly towards her, weaving through the air like a wide brown satin ribbon. It swirled around her, encircling her hips and thighs, and then moulded itself to her body. Caitlyn gasped as she felt the warm chocolate touch her skin. But it didn't feel like chocolate—instead, it felt like a satin sheet, smoothing itself to her curves. And within minutes, she felt the silky chocolate cool and harden, forming a flexible dark sheath which encased her waist, tummy, hips, and thighs. It flattened her stomach, smoothed her thighs, and tightened her hips and bottom, giving her a sleek hourglass figure. Caitlyn laughed in disbelief. It was like chocolate spandex!

Then the Widow Mags flicked her other hand and the green dress floated through the air, slipped over Caitlyn's head, and settled itself gracefully around her body, fitting her perfectly.

"That's... that's *amazing!*" Caitlyn spluttered. She laughed. "Pomona is going to die when she hears this—imagine using *chocolate* to make you look thinner!" Impulsively, she reached over and kissed the Widow Mags on the cheek. "Thank you!"

"All right, all right... don't fuss," said the Widow Mags gruffly, although her eyes were bright with pleasure. Then she became serious and wagged a finger at Caitlyn. "There *is* one condition you need to remember..."

"Don't tell me, it turns into a pumpkin on the stroke of afternoon tea?" said Caitlyn with a laugh, too excited to care.

"No," said the Widow Mags. "However, the chocolate sheath can melt if you're not careful. Not from your body heat—it is enchanted so that it won't melt on contact with your skin—but it is attuned to your *emotional* temperature."

"My emotional temperature?" said Caitlyn, puzzled.

"Yes. If you become agitated for any reason, if your heart beats faster and your pulse races— whether from excitement, fear, or anger—the chocolate will begin to melt."

"So hang on to your temper!" said Bertha with a chuckle. "Not the easiest thing for a redhead."

Caitlyn smoothed the dress down over her flat stomach and smiled. "Don't worry, I'm going to be the most zen person at the party!"

CHAPTER TWENTY

Caitlyn arrived at the Garden Party really feeling a bit like Cinderella. As she joined the crowd milling around the landscaped front gardens of Huntingdon Manor, she saw several people eyeing her admiringly and her confidence soared. She accepted a glass of Pimms—that quintessential English summer cocktail—from a waiter walking past with a silver tray, and then set out to mingle.

Whatever James's worries might have been, it looked like everything had come together for the party wonderfully. Pretty, pastel-coloured streamers and bunting were draped everywhere, lending an elegant, festive feel to the occasion. Wicker chairs and colourful cushions had been scattered about the garden, and picnic blankets were spread beneath several trees. A string quartet played softly in one shady corner and, across the lawn from it, several men in polo shirts and women in floaty floral dresses played croquet on the perfectly manicured grass.

A long row of trestle tables had been set up in the centre of the front gardens, covered with a pristine white cloth and displaying an array of vintage teapots and porcelain china teacups. These were accompanied by a smorgasbord of English picnic foods: loaves of freshly-baked bread, cold smoked meats, potato salad, sausage rolls, dainty finger sandwiches, Scotch eggs, creamy cheeses, classic pork pie, and Cornish pasties. And if that wasn't enough, there was dessert to follow in the shape of scones with home-made jam and clotted cream, traditional fruitcake, juicy fresh strawberries and—last but not least—chocolate treats from *Bewitched by Chocolate*.

In the centre of the table, taking pride of place, was the Widow Mags's magnificent chocolate fudge cake, surrounded by piles of her home-made fudge, decadent chocolate truffles, gourmet chocolate bars, and other cocoa sweets. Caitlyn couldn't help noticing, though, that no one was helping themselves to any of the chocolate. People were making a wide detour around that section of the table and eyeing all the chocolates warily. A few looked more wistful than fearful but even they didn't seem to have the courage to go up and try a piece. The beautifully crafted chocolates, fudge,

197

cake, and other treats sat forlornly, untouched, melting slightly in the sun.

Caitlyn glanced across the lawn at the Widow Mags, who was standing by herself, trying to look unbothered, and felt her heart go out to the old witch. She knew that it must hurt the Widow Mags to see all her hard work and careful preparation being snubbed by the villagers. A middle-aged woman with stiff permed hair walked past the old witch and smiled smugly, and Caitlyn felt a surge of anger at Winifred Harris. It seemed that the malicious woman had done her job and convinced everyone to cold-shoulder the Widow Mags and her chocolates.

Caitlyn was about to walk over to offer her support when a tall, thin woman, with an upturned nose and a bit too much make-up, sauntered past. Their eyes met and Angela Skinner's mouth dropped open as she surveyed Caitlyn's appearance.

"Hi, Angela," Caitlyn said with a smile.

"Caitlyn!" The other woman's eyes bulged. "You... you look fabulous..." she said, sounding like the words were choking her.

"Thank you," Caitlyn's smile grew wider. "You deserve the credit for that—if you hadn't picked out this beautiful dress for me—"

"And does it... er... fit okay?" asked Angela, her eyes hard and suspicious.

"Oh yes," said Caitlyn, smoothing her hands

down over her hips. "It fits perfectly. Almost as if it was made for me—it's really done wonders for my figure."

Angela gave her a look of angry frustration, then offered a sickly smile before turning and stalking away. Caitlyn swallowed a laugh. It was petty and childish, she knew, to be gloating over Angela's discomfiture, but there was something so nice about seeing the other woman thwarted.

She turned back to where the Widow Mags had been standing but the old witch was no longer there. Caitlyn frowned, scanning the crowds, but she couldn't see the old woman anywhere. She looked for Pomona too and finally saw her cousin in the distance, standing with a group of fashionably dressed young guests who looked like London professionals. They were talking and laughing uproariously together, and looked like they were having a great time.

Caitlyn was just starting to make her way across the lawn towards them when she heard her name being called by a familiar deep voice.

"Caitlyn."

She turned to see James Fitzroy approaching her, looking ridiculously handsome and the epitome of the English gentleman in a tailored linen jacket paired with a crisp white shirt, the top buttons undone to reveal the bronzed column of his neck and chest.

James smiled at her, his grey eyes admiring.

"You look beautiful."

Caitlyn flushed. "Th-thanks, you look pretty stunning yourself... Oh! I mean... I'm not—"

He laughed easily. "No, please, don't take it back. My ego would be crushed."

"The... um... the party is great," she said hurriedly. "The place looks fantastic and everyone seems to be really enjoying themselves."

"Yes, I'm glad now that I didn't cancel the event. It's all down to the hard work, of course, of my staff. I thought—"

"Lord Fitzroy."

They turned to see Inspector Walsh standing next to them. "I'm sorry to interrupt, sir, but it is a matter of some urgency."

"Yes, Inspector?" James looked at him inquiringly.

"As you know, we have been checking the bank accounts of the various suspects. We noticed that there have been several large sums of money leaving Matt O'Brien's account at regular intervals in the past few months. Always cash withdrawals. They may be nothing but they do look suspicious. We'd like to question Mr O'Brien again. My men have been looking for him this morning but we haven't been able to locate him. Do you know where he might be?"

"Now that you mention it, I haven't seen him all morning either, which is a bit odd," said James with a frown. "I would have thought that he would be here with the other gardeners, helping out..." Then he brightened. "He might have gone into Cheltenham last night and not returned yet. I've heard from Old Palmer that Matt likes his drink and can sometimes have a 'big night out'. He's complained about Matt turning up late for work with a hangover the next day."

Inspector Walsh turned to Caitlyn. "And you, Miss Le Fey? Do you have any ideas where he might be? I understand that your cousin has become very... *ahem*... friendly with the Irishman."

Caitlyn shifted uncomfortably. "I have no idea," she said honestly. "And I haven't spoken to Pomie yet today so I don't know about her."

"It is imperative that we speak to Mr O'Brien... and to make sure that he has not left the area."

James looked at him in surprise. "Are you suggesting that Matt might have done a bunk?"

The inspector inclined his head. "It would not be the first time a suspect has escaped before his guilt could be proven."

"But... but I just don't understand why Matt would want to kill my housekeeper," said James. "I mean, he doesn't have any motive!"

Caitlyn bit her lip, wondering what to do. She glanced across the lawn at Pomona in the distance and remembered her promise to her cousin—but on the other hand, if Matt really was the murderer and she didn't speak up, she would never be able to live with that on her conscience.

"Actually..." She cleared her throat and the two men looked at her questioningly. "Matt could have a motive—a very strong motive for killing Mrs Brixton..." Quickly, she told them about discovering the hidden cannabis plants in the greenhouse.

"Growing cannabis in my greenhouse?" said James incredulously.

Caitlyn nodded. "I think Mrs Brixton must have found out about it and used it to blackmail Matt."

"And when were you planning to inform us of this interesting piece of information, Miss Le Fey?" asked the inspector icily.

She flushed. "I... I was going to come and tell you, Inspector. I just got a bit... um... side-tracked. And anyway, I didn't think it would matter much... one more day—"

"*Didn't think it would matter much?*" the inspector's voice turned furious. "It could mean the difference between the murderer being convicted or getting away! Withholding information that is pertinent to a murder investigation is a serious offence, young lady. I hope for your sake that your reticence hasn't cost us an arrest!"

Turning, he gave terse commands to two of his men, instructing them to search the grounds for Matt, then he stalked off in the direction of the Manor. Caitlyn swallowed and looked down, not wanting to meet James's eyes. There was an uncomfortable silence.

Finally, James cleared his throat and said with a

sympathetic smile, "Sometimes it can be hard to do the right thing. It was Pomona, wasn't it? She asked you not to tell the police about Matt."

Caitlyn nodded. "She said that the police were prejudiced against Matt because of his past criminal record and that they'd jump on him and use him as a scapegoat for the murder." She sighed. "But it was my fault too. I shouldn't have let her talk me into it..."

"You could have come and told *me*, Caitlyn," said James softly. "You should have trusted me."

"I..." Caitlyn stared up into his warm grey eyes and felt her heart flutter. Then she remembered her chocolate spandex. *Mustn't get hot and bothered, mustn't get hot and bothered*, she told herself frantically.

She was almost relieved when a movement near them distracted James's attention. He glanced over at the long table, then his brows drew together.

"Nobody seems to be eating the chocolates," he said with a frown.

Caitlyn followed his gaze. "Yes," she said with a sigh. "People are scared of the Widow Mags and her creations... and there are... um... some individuals who have been deliberately encouraging that fear and prejudice."

As they watched, a lone figure finally approached the table and went up to the chocolates. It was Molly. The little girl was wearing a pretty white dress and colourful ribbons on her pigtails. She reached up eagerly towards a chocolate lollipop, but just as her chubby fingers closed around the lollipop stick, a woman rushed up and slapped it out of her hands.

"I told you never to touch those chocolates, Molly!" cried the young woman. "They are from that witch's shop!"

"But Mummy, she's a good witch—" the little girl started to protest before her mother cut her off.

"They're evil and bewitched! You're not to eat any of those chocolates, do you hear me?" She grabbed the little girl's hand and hauled her away, with Molly still protesting.

"This is ridiculous," said James, his lips tightening.

He strode over to the table and Caitlyn hurried after him. She felt everyone's eyes on them—even the string quartet seemed to pause in their playing to watch. James reached out and picked up a large piece of chocolate fudge from the top of the pile nearest to him. As the entire village watched, he raised it to his mouth and bit into the square of rich, creamy chocolate confectionery.

"Absolutely delicious," he said loudly, smacking his lips with relish.

Caitlyn was touched by his gesture. And she could see that already, several of the villagers were drifting closer, their curiosity and desire for the chocolate overcoming their wariness.

"D'you feel alright, Lord Fitzroy?" one of them

asked.

"Of course! Why wouldn't I?" asked James. He picked up a chocolate truffle from the table and popped it into his mouth, closing his eyes in ecstasy. "Mmm.... These are *incredible.*"

More and more people were drifting towards the table now and several were beginning to reach hesitantly towards the chocolates. One man looked furtively around, then picked up a piece of chocolate fudge and bit into one corner. His expression was almost comical as he tasted it. His eyes bulged, then softened and went dreamy, and a wide smile spread across his face. He crammed the rest of the piece into his mouth and reached eagerly for another. Next to him, a woman picked up one of the gourmet chocolate bars—a solid oblong of creamy milk chocolate with roasted hazelnuts embedded in the surface, which Caitlyn recognised as one she had helped make. The woman nibbled the edge of the bar, then gasped "Oh! Ohhh!" and broke into a wide grin. She scoffed the rest of the bar in two seconds and began eyeing the chocolate truffles.

James picked up another piece of chocolate fudge and turned to Caitlyn with a smile. "You're not having any."

Caitlyn hesitated, then reached out and took the fudge from him. She was very aware of their fingers brushing and tried to cover it up by quickly taking a bite. For a moment she forgot James, the party, everything, as the intense, bittersweet flavours filled her mouth and she savoured the dense, creamy texture of the rich, chocolatey fudge.

"Oops—you've got some crumbs on your..." James chuckled and pointed discreetly at her mouth.

"Oh..." Caitlyn flushed and hurriedly brushed at her lips.

"No, the other side." James made a movement, then stopped himself. "A bit lower..."

Caitlyn tried unsuccessfully to find the crumbs.

"If... if you'll allow me..." James cleared his throat, then reached out and gently brushed his thumb at the corner of her lips.

Caitlyn froze, her breath catching in her throat. He seemed suddenly very close, his face bent towards hers, his eyes intent on her lips. She felt as if every sense was on fire—she could smell the clean, male scent of him; she was aware of the warmth emanating from his body; she could feel the rough pad of his thumb against the soft skin of her lips—and her heart pounded like a mad thing.

Then she became aware of something else—a warm, sticky, unpleasant feeling. It took her a moment to realise that it was around her hips and thighs, and then she felt her dress suddenly tighten and strain across her belly. She gasped in horror as she realised what was happening.

Her chocolate spandex was melting!

CHAPTER TWENTY-ONE

.

Caitlyn jerked back from James, her mind frantically remembering the Widow Mags's warning, and felt the chocolate body sheath melt even more. Her agitation was only making it worse, and with every moment that passed, she could feel her dress getting tighter and tighter, as the control shapewear properties of the magical chocolate mould began disappearing.

No, no, no! she thought in a panic, wrapping her arms around her middle.

"Caitlyn? Is something the matter?" James looked puzzled.

"Um... no... sorry, I... I've got to go!" she mumbled, shuffling away.

She pushed through the crowd, looking desperately around. She needed to find the Widow

Mags and ask her to fix the chocolate mould. But she couldn't see the old witch anywhere. And the more she stumbled around, frantically searching, the worse things got. She could feel the melting chocolate start to ooze down her thighs now.

Abandoning the search for the Widow Mags, Caitlyn shuffled towards the Manor. If she could just find somewhere private where she could calm herself down and maybe adjust her clothing, she might still be able to salvage things... She spied the side door that she had entered the other day with the kitten and quickly hurried inside. The darkened hallway was blessedly cool and Caitlyn felt her pulse slow slightly. She stepped through the first door she saw and found herself back in the Steward's Office, where she had been trapped under the desk by an affectionate Bran.

Her eyes lit up as she saw the antique lacquered Chinese screen in the far corner. Quickly, she crossed the room and ducked behind the screen. She hitched her dress up around the waist and looked down to inspect the damage. *Okay, okay, it isn't too bad*, she told herself. The chocolate sheath had lost some of its shape but it was already cooling and hardening again. It was still malleable, though, so if she just pulled it back up and pressed it back into place, it would probably re-mould to the contours of her body.

She sucked her stomach in and tugged the chocolate sheath upwards, smoothing her hands over it and pressing it against her hips and thighs. But it remained loose and floppy. Caitlyn felt a flutter of panic again. *This had to work!*

Taking a deep breath, she closed her eyes and concentrated hard, remembering what the Widow Mags had told her: *"...magic is simply the ability to cause change by force of will..."*

She tried again, pressing her hands down on the chocolate, *willing* it to mould to her body. Then... with a thrill, she felt it: the chocolate changed texture, becoming satiny and cool again. It tightened and firmed around her, flattening her stomach, slimming her hips and thighs.

Then she heard the door to the room open and someone step in. Caitlyn froze. The last thing she needed was for one of the guests to find her here, with her dress hitched up around her midriff and her hips and thighs encased in weird chocolate underwear! What if the story got back to James?

She could feel her heart start to thud in her chest again and had to force herself to remain calm. There was no reason for anyone to realise that she was here behind the screen, she reminded herself. There was no gap along the bottom or between the panels and, as long as she made no noise, no one would know. Hopefully whoever it was would get what they wanted and leave quickly.

Then she realised that the person who just entered the room didn't sound calm either. She could hear their quick, hurried breathing and, although she couldn't see, she sensed a furtiveness in their presence. They shut the door quietly, then moved softly across the room. Caitlyn heard the jingle of keys, then a *click*, followed by a hoarse creaking. And then the rustle of papers.

Her curiosity getting the better of her, Caitlyn inched to the edge of the screen and peered cautiously around it. She blinked in surprise to see Winifred Harris hunched over the antique desk on the other side of the room, which now had its slanted top open. Thankfully, the woman was turned away from her—she was bending over the open compartment of the desk and muttering to herself as she rifled through the pages of an old leather-bound ledger.

There was a pause, then Caitlyn heard the sound of paper ripping, followed by more page turning, and then the ripping again. This was repeated several times. Then Mrs Harris stuffed several torn pages into her handbag, slammed the ledger shut, and slid it back into the compartment. She lowered the slanted hinged top into place and pulled a bunch of keys out of her handbag to lock it.

Caitlyn stifled a gasp, her eyes riveted on the keys. She had seen a bunch of keys exactly like that recently: a big, old-fashioned ring with lots of keys hanging from it, just like the ones Victorian housekeepers used to carry. She had seen it being carried by Mrs Brixton and then lying on the coffee table when she had dropped off her wet clothes in the housekeeper's sitting room. It was the same bunch of keys that had been missing when she had returned with the police to the scene of murder. She tried to remember if Inspector Walsh had mentioned finding the keys—no, there had been no mention of them at all since that first day. It was almost as if it had been forgotten in all the excitement about the theft of the bloodstone ring.

But if that *was* the same ring of keys, what was Mrs Harris doing with it?

The woman turned from the desk and Caitlyn hastily jerked out of sight behind the screen. She held her breath and listened as footsteps crossed the room again. There was the sound of the door opening and closing—and then silence descended in the room once more.

Caitlyn let out her breath and peeked out from behind the screen again, then relaxed. Hastily, she smoothed her dress back down over her body and stepped out into the empty room. She approached the antique writing desk and ran a hand along its faded surface. What had Winifred Harris been doing? Caitlyn tried to raise the lid but found it securely locked. She bent and examined the lock. It was an old-fashioned warded lock with the traditional keyhole made to fit those big brass "skeleton" keys.

Then, before she had time to react, she heard a new step in the hallway outside. The next moment, the door swung open and Pomona stepped into the room, looking fabulous in a white sundress with a halter-neck top that showed off her golden tan.

"You're here! I've been looking everywhere for you. I was just gonna ask James to put out an announcement when someone told me they saw you coming in this side door—" She broke off as she registered Caitlyn's expression. "What?"

"Nothing." Caitlyn breathed a sigh of relief. "I thought you were Mrs Harris coming back."

"Who's Mrs Harris...? Oh, not that old busybody on the village committee who goes around telling everyone what to do?" Pomona made a face.

"She might be something else as well..." Caitlyn said darkly.

"What d'you mean?"

"She was in here just now and she had a bunch of keys with her—the same bunch of keys that used to belong to Mrs Brixton, and which went missing after the murder."

Pomona's eyes widened. "You mean..."

"I don't know," said Caitlyn. "I know it sounds crazy but... maybe... maybe Winifred Harris is the murderer? Otherwise, why would she have the keys?"

"But... are you saying that she murdered the housekeeper just to get her hands on some keys?" Pomona looked sceptical. "Couldn't she have just, like, stolen them, made copies, and then put them back?"

Caitlyn shrugged. "Maybe the murder happened

for other reasons. But it's definitely suspicious that she's got the keys."

"What was she doing with them?"

"She used them to open that," said Caitlyn, pointing to the antique writing desk. "She took out a big leather-bound book—I think it was an accounts ledger because I remember James saying the other day that Mrs Brixton kept a lot of the household accounting in that desk—and then she ripped out some pages from it."

"Really?" Pomona's eyes were bright with curiosity now. She approached the desk and bent down to examine the lock, like Caitlyn had done earlier. "Hmm..."

"I suppose we could go and ask James for the key," said Caitlyn hesitantly. "I'm sure he must have duplicate copies of everything. But I wish we could open it and check first. I mean, I don't really know how to explain it to him... Wouldn't it sound like I'm accusing Mrs Harris? And what if she was in here for a legitimate reason? Ugh, that would be so embarrassing..." She joined Pomona by the desk and crouched down in front of the keyhole again, then sighed impatiently. "I wish I knew a spell to unlock it!"

Pomona grinned suddenly and elbowed Caitlyn out of the way. "Maybe we don't need a spell."

"What do you mean?"

Her cousin didn't answer. Instead, Pomona reached up and pulled something out of her hair. It was a large satin flower with a giant bobby pin attached. She removed the pin, straightened it, then carefully applied pressure at one end to bend it into the shape of a hook, then again at the other end so that it formed a short L-shaped handle. Then she crouched down in front of the keyhole and slowly inserted the pin into the hole, jiggling it gently while also turning it at the same time.

A minute later, there came a faint *click* and Pomona smiled triumphantly as she lifted the lid on the desk.

CHAPTER TWENTY-TWO

"That's amazing!" said Caitlyn. "How did you learn to do that?"

Pomona shrugged. "You pick up these things in your teens."

"I never learned to do stuff like that."

Her cousin grinned. "I told you—you didn't go to the right parties."

Both girls looked into the compartment beneath the slant-topped lid of the desk. There were several old leather-bound volumes. Caitlyn picked up the one at the top of the pile and flipped through it. They could immediately see that several pages had been ripped out.

"I saw Mrs Harris removing some of these pages," said Caitlyn. "I wonder why she did that?"

Pomona tilted her head, trying to read the

handwritten entries on the remaining pages. "It looks like a bunch of expenses..." She followed a couple of lines with her finger. "They look like things for a party."

"Yeah, I think this is a record of all the expenses from the Garden Party each year, as well as a few other events that the Manor organises with the village committee. This must be a separate account dedicated to funding those expenses," said Caitlyn. "Look, these last pages are for this year's party..." She trailed off and frowned. "It looks like Winifred Harris ripped some pages out of each year's party expenses."

"What did she do with them?"

"She stuffed them in her handbag and took them with her."

"What for?"

Caitlyn shook her head helplessly. "I don't know. The only thing I can think of is... she wanted to remove the record of those expenses... but why?"

"I know! 'Cos they were faked," said Pomona suddenly. "I'll bet you anything that's why Mrs Harris snuck in here: to remove evidence of her embezzling money from the Manor account. And— hey! If Mrs Brixton was in charge of these accounts, then she must have been in on it too!"

"Yes, you could be right," Caitlyn said excitedly. "And that might explain something else: the motive for the murder! We know Mrs Brixton was really into blackmailing people—she'd already tried it with

Amelia and with Matt O'Brien too—so maybe she saw this as a golden opportunity to blackmail Mrs Harris as well."

"Oh yeah, she probably said she would tell James and everyone else in the village about the fake expenses—unless Mrs Harris paid up." Pomona wrinkled her nose. "And that Harris woman is such a pompous, self-righteous snob—she'd kill anyone who tried to mess with her reputation. Like, literally."

Caitlyn thought about it for a second. "I'm not sure that she actually planned it, you know. I think... I wonder if... if maybe the whole thing was an accident."

"An accident?"

"Yes. I mean, I'm sure you're right: Mrs Brixton *did* try to blackmail Mrs Harris exactly like you said... but maybe... maybe the two of them got into a fight that day. Mrs Harris was already in a bad mood because she'd just been trying to remove the Widow Mags's chocolates from the Garden Party menu and James refused. I was there when she came to see him. She must have already been seething. And then... she must have gone to see Mrs Brixton after that. I just thought she went home when she stormed out, but actually she went to search for the housekeeper. In fact..." Caitlyn frowned in an effort to remember. "When I went back to the old servants' quarters to collect my clothes, I remember hearing raised voices in Mrs

Brixton's sitting room. The door was closed so I didn't see who it was, but it sounded like they were having an argument."

"Wait... are you saying that Harris killed the housekeeper by mistake?"

Caitlyn nodded. "She's got a terrible temper. You should have seen her last night at the chocolate shop—she didn't like something the Widow Mags said so she grabbed a jar of chocolate sauce nearby and looked like she wanted to smash it on someone's skull!"

"Jeez..." said Pomona, shaking her head. "Sounds like she's got anger management issues."

"That's what I thought too. And you know, I think that's what happened with Mrs Brixton! They were arguing, Mrs Harris lost her temper, grabbed the nearest thing—which happened to be that big china jug—and hit the housekeeper on the head with it. And then when she realised that Mrs Brixton was dead... maybe she just panicked and ran away."

"She didn't panic that much if she remembered to take the keys," said Pomona. "That means that she was cool enough to think about damage control."

"What do you mean?"

"Well, if she got rid of the record of those fake expenses, then she'd be removing all evidence of her embezzling activities, right? And with Mrs Brixton dead, no one else would know. The whole thing would be buried."

Caitlyn snapped her fingers. "You know what? You're right. And I think that's what she was trying to do yesterday! She came in here when James and I were in the office and she looked taken aback to find us. At the time, I thought she was just snooping around—you know, for village gossip—but now I think she was probably trying to get to the ledger. She must have been really frustrated to find us here, which meant she had to abandon her plan—"

"But she decided to try again today when there would be a lot more people around, and it'd be easier to sneak in here unnoticed!" Pomona finished for her.

Caitlyn nodded. She picked up the ledger and shut the desk again. "Come on—we've got to tell James and the police!"

Hugging the ledger to her chest, Caitlyn left the room with Pomona at her heels. But they had barely stepped out of the office when they heard a terrified scream. They looked at each other in surprise, then rushed outside, hurrying across the gravel driveway that circled the front of the Manor and into the formal gardens beyond. But they stopped short as they reached the front lawns and stared in horror at the scene in front of them.

Inspector Walsh and a few of his men were standing in a semicircle around Matt O'Brien, who was glaring at them with a defiant expression on his face. He had one arm wrapped tightly around the little girl, Molly, and in his other hand he held a pair of pruning shears, open so that the sharp edges were directed towards the child.

Pomona gasped and rushed forwards. "Matt! What are you doing?"

"Don't hurt her... please!" sobbed Molly's mother, standing at the edge of the crowd which had gathered around the scene.

"Then tell the fecking police not to come any closer!" Matt snarled. He looked terrible, his jaw unshaven and his eyes bloodshot, and his normally handsome features distorted with panic and desperation.

Inspector Walsh held his hands up, palms forward, and said in a carefully neutral voice, "Now, let's calm down, sir. We just want to ask you a few questions—"

"A few questions, my arse!" spat Matt. "You want to arrest me! I know you think I murdered Brixton. I didn't kill her but I know you won't believe me. You'll just look at my record and assume: once a criminal, always a criminal! Well, I'm telling you now, I'm not going back inside!"

"Matt, don't do this," begged Pomona. "I believed you, right? I know you didn't murder Mrs Brixton. I'll speak to the police for you. I've got contacts—I know this really good attorney in Hollywood—I'm sure we can—"

Matt gave a mirthless laugh. "It's no use,

gorgeous. Thanks for the vote of confidence but I'm not taking my chances. I'll do this my way."

Pomona looked at him angrily. "By using a child as a hostage? You're a pathetic coward!"

Matt shrugged. "Sorry to disappoint you, sweetheart, but I've never pretended to be a saint. I'm only doing what anyone else would in my position—looking after my own skin."

Inspector Walsh tried again. "If you can just let the child go, sir, we can discuss this at your—"

Matt gave a jeering laugh. "Let her go? Not bloody likely! She's my ticket to getting out of here. I should never have come back from Cheltenham..." he muttered to himself. He raised the pruning shears. "You want to keep her safe? You keep your distance!" He made a threatening motion and Molly flinched and cried out.

Molly's mother gasped and James Fitzroy made a compulsive movement forwards, but Matt swung suddenly in his direction and jabbed the shears in the air.

"Not so fast, your lordship! I wouldn't want to hurt you—I've always liked you—you've been fair with me and I respect that. But I won't hesitate if you try anything."

"Matt, let the child go—you're scaring her," said James in a calm, reasonable voice. He shifted his feet as he spoke, inching slowly forwards.

Caitlyn wondered if he was thinking of tackling the gardener. But would he be able to move fast enough to disarm Matt? And what about Molly? The way the little girl was being held, like a shield in front of Matt's body, she would probably get caught in the middle. Caitlyn looked at the sharp edge of the pruning shears gleaming in Matt's hand and shuddered at the thought of the blade cutting the child by mistake. It was too much of a risk. She glanced at James and could see from the grim expression on his face that he had come to the same conclusion.

Matt narrowed his eyes and looked at the men encircling him. "Now, I'm going to walk out of here, nice and easy, and I don't want any sudden moves or anyone trying to follow me. If you do as I say, I won't hurt the child. But if you try anything funny..." He made another threatening motion with the shears towards the little girl's neck.

Molly's mother screamed and put out her hands wildly. "Do as he says! Do as he says!" she sobbed.

Inspector Walsh hesitated, then made a terse gesture towards his men. They fell back reluctantly, moving so that the Irishman had an open path to escape. Pomona made a frustrated noise in her throat but she too stood back and watched helplessly as Matt gripped the little girl tightly and prepared to leave.

CHAPTER TWENTY-THREE

Matt began backing away from them, still holding Molly in front of him. He relaxed slightly as he saw that everyone was following his instructions and no one was attempting to stop him.

"Yeah, that's right..." He nodded approvingly, continuing to back away.

The long table was in his path and, to get to the gravel driveway, he would have to go around it. He adjusted his hold on Molly and started moving sideways along the table. As he passed the section of the table where the chocolates were displayed, he paused and glanced at the stacks of chocolate fudge, inhaling their rich aroma.

"Grab me a piece," he told Molly.

The little girl reached out a trembling hand and picked up a square of chocolate fudge, then turned and placed it in Matt's waiting mouth. He chewed appreciatively.

"Mm... that's grand. I'm almost sorry not to be hanging around to eat more of this." He gave a mocking laugh, his usual cocky manner returning. "I can take a couple more for the road, though..."

Just as he was about to tell Molly to get more fudge, a hunched figure stepped suddenly out of the crowd: an old woman with a large hooked nose, fierce eyebrows, and wispy grey hair pulled back in a bun. She was wearing a long black dress that looked completely at odds with the rest of the floral dresses and summer outfits that the other guests were wearing. It was the Widow Mags.

She glowered at Matt from across the lawn. "Release the child now," she said, her voice carrying across the open space.

Matt looked bemused for a moment, then he gave a bark of laughter. "Are you talking to me, old woman? Think you're really a witch, eh? What are you going to do? Turn me into a toad?" He gave another jeering laugh.

The Widow Mags's eyes flashed and she raised her arms suddenly. In a terrible voice, she intoned:

Dormant creatures,
Of magic partake;
Heed my words,
Arise and awake!

The villagers looked wildly around, as if expecting a crack of thunder or a flash of lightning from the sky, but Caitlyn remembered those words. She looked sharply at the chocolate fudge cake, where suddenly a dozen wings fluttered to life. The next moment, a cloud of chocolate-coloured butterflies lifted from the surface of cake and took to the air.

"What the—?" Matt looked up uncertainly as the butterflies circled above his head. Then, without warning, they swarmed around him. They darted in and out, swooping close, diving at his eyes, attacking his face.

"*Aaah!*" he cried, letting go of the girl and slapping wildly at his own face. "Feck! Get away from me! Get away!"

The moment Matt's grip loosened on Molly, James saw his chance. He dived forwards, grabbing the little girl's arm and yanking her away, turning so that he shielded her with his body as they hit the ground and rolled over.

"Seize him!" cried Inspector Walsh and the constables surged forwards, surrounding Matt.

A few minutes later, it was all over. The police stood around a subdued Matt O'Brien, his hand twisted behind his back in handcuffs, whilst Molly's mother hugged the little girl to her chest and sobbed with relief.

"Matt O'Brien," said the inspector, his voice carrying across the gardens, "I'm arresting you for the murder of Mrs Brixton—"

"No, wait!" cried Caitlyn, stepping forwards. "He's not the murderer."

Everyone turned to gape at her.

"I beg your pardon, Miss Le Fey?" said Inspector Walsh, frowning at her.

Caitlyn took a deep breath. "I don't think Matt O'Brien murdered Mrs Brixton."

"Caitlyn, what are you saying?" demanded James. "You told me yourself that Matt had good reason for murdering Mrs Brixton because she was blackmailing him about his secret cannabis crop—"

"Yes, I know—and I still think she was. But she was blackmailing someone else too—someone who *also* had very good reason to murder her. And who I believe *is* the person who killed her." Caitlyn swung around and pointed at a middle-aged woman with a stiff permed hairdo standing at the edge of the crowd. "Mrs Harris."

The woman gave a gasp of outrage. "How dare you!"

Confused murmurs rose from the crowd around them. People couldn't believe Caitlyn's accusation. Winifred Harris was one of the most well-known and highly regarded village residents.

James frowned and moved closer to Caitlyn, lowering his voice. "Are you sure? Mrs Harris is a respected member of the village. She serves on several committees and local councils. This is a serious allegation."

"And that's exactly why she murdered Mrs Brixton," said Caitlyn, raising her voice so that everyone could hear her. "She had too much to lose: her standing in the community, her reputation, her very identity—Mrs Brixton was threatening to destroy all that by telling people the truth."

"What truth?" asked James.

"Don't listen to her, Lord Fitzroy!" snapped Winifred Harris. "She's... she's just trying to protect her own skin! She's a suspect for the murder herself, isn't she? Everyone knows she was seen lurking around the Manor just at the time the murder took place, even though she denies it."

"Caitlyn had an alibi!" Pomona said indignantly. "She left the Manor and was walking back to the chocolate shop. There's, like, a witness who can confirm they saw her at the stone circle."

"Not the last time I heard," said Mrs Harris, glancing across at Angela. "In any case, it would have been easy for Miss Le Fey to make sure that she was seen on the hill, even when she was still back at the Manor, murdering Mrs Brixton."

"How on earth would I have done that?" asked Caitlyn in exasperation.

"By witchcraft!" Mrs Harris hissed, narrowing her eyes.

There were audible gasps and muted cries from the crowd and Caitlyn saw several pairs of hostile eyes turn towards her. Winifred Harris saw the reactions too and pressed her advantage. She took a step forwards, her voice becoming sanctimonious.

"Yes, witchcraft! That girl is a witch—just like the old woman! Yesterday, I caught her trying to corrupt one of the children in the village... little Molly here! She was trying to tempt the child with some of the evil bewitched chocolates from the shop... And now she's here, accusing me of the vilest crime! Me? Me, whom all of you have known for years? My family have lived and worked in Tillyhenge for generations. And who is she? A stranger, an interloper sent here to do evil and taint your minds!"

Caitlyn looked helplessly around. She could see from people's faces that Winifred Harris's words were beginning to take effect. The villagers were eyeing her now with suspicion and resentment. Her heart sank. This had become a case of her word against Mrs Harris's and she knew that she couldn't hope to win. The other woman had years of trust and familiarity on her side, whereas Caitlyn was an outsider—an outsider, moreover, who lived with "the village witch".

She looked pleadingly at Inspector Walsh, hoping that the police might support her. "Inspector, you've got to believe me. She was in the Manor just now, with the ring of keys that Mrs Brixton had—the same ring of keys that went missing on the day of the murder. How could she have those keys, unless she was somehow involved with the murder? And she was using them to—"

"I'm not listening to this nonsense any longer!" Mrs Harris tossed her head. "I'm leaving!"

She turned and began stalking towards the gravel driveway, her head held high, but she hadn't gone a few steps when two shapes bounded out of the bushes nearby: a little ball of black fluff, followed by a large lumbering beast. It was Nibs the kitten and Bran the mastiff, and they looked like they were playing a game of chase. They gambolled out into the open space, oblivious to the stares of the crowd, and right into Winifred Harris's path. The middle-aged woman cried out as the kitten darted between her ankles, then she stumbled, tripped, and fell onto her face on the lawn.

"Mrs Harris!" James hurried forwards to help her.

The woman had dropped her handbag and the contents had spilled out onto the grass beside her. She lay stunned for a moment, then scrambled to her knees and began hurriedly collecting her spilled possessions.

James crouched down next to her. "Here, let me help—"

"No, no... Thank you, Lord Fitzroy... there's really no need... I can manage..." She babbled, grabbing things frantically and shoving them back into her bag. She reached for a sheaf of papers but James picked them up before she did.

"What are these?" he asked with a frown, unfolding the papers and smoothing them out.

Mrs Harris went pale. "They're... er..."

"They're ripped from your ledger book!" Pomona shouted. "Caitlyn saw her do it. She ripped them out so that nobody would know she's been skimming money off the Garden Party expense account!"

The crowd was silent, stunned. Then Caitlyn stepped forwards.

"It's true. I saw Mrs Harris in the Steward's Office just now. She unlocked the writing desk and took out one of the ledgers—the one for the Garden Party account expenses—and tore some of the pages out. And the keys she used to open the desk were from the ring last seen with Mrs Brixton before she was murdered."

"This is... ridiculous! Ridiculous!" Mrs Harris looked wildly around at the other faces in the crowd. "Surely you don't believe her? It's the most ludicrous suggestion I have ever heard! Mrs Brixton was my friend—I'd known her for years—why would I want to kill her?"

"Because she wasn't really your friend—she was your partner-in-crime. The two of you must have been in collusion, claiming hundreds, maybe thousands of extra pounds every year from the Fitzroy estate in false expenses," said Caitlyn.

"Lies! All lies!" Winifred Harris spluttered.

Caitlyn ignored her. "But then Mrs Brixton probably got greedy. She decided that not only was she going to keep getting money from the estate, she'd also get some extra money off you as well! She started trying to blackmail you and you couldn't bear it—that's why you killed her. To silence her and protect your own reputa—"

"I didn't *plan* to kill her!" Mrs Harris cried, her face red. "It just happened! It was an accident!"

There was a shocked silence from the crowd.

Mrs Harris raised a trembling hand to her mouth as she realised what she had blurted out. "I... I mean..."

James stepped forwards, looking at her sternly. "Mrs Harris, I think you have a lot of explaining to do..."

CHAPTER TWENTY-FOUR

"Oh, no you don't," said Pomona, reaching into the back seat of her convertible and lifting out a wriggling bundle of black fur. "You're not gonna try that trick again! I can't have you stowing away to London—I don't wanna have to turn around just to bring you back."

She set the kitten down on the gravel driveway and Nibs gave himself a shake, making the bell on his collar tinkle, before trotting off to join Bran the mastiff, who was stretched out in the shade of a nearby tree.

Pomona chuckled as she watched the kitten scamper away and said, "On second thoughts, maybe I should just take him with me. He's so cute—I bet he'd be a big hit at this premiere."

Caitlyn laughed. "I can just imagine the news

coverage now—all these glamorous celebrities on the red carpet... and then this little black kitten tripping them up!"

Pomona grinned. "It would make a change from the usual boring routine. Seriously, people think these premieres and parties are so exciting but it's the same people half the time and all they wanna do is talk about themselves or show the paparazzi that they're wearing some dress with no underwear."

"But you love it really," said Caitlyn with a laugh. She'd seen Pomona in news clips and gracing photos in celebrity magazines, hobnobbing with Hollywood stars at the latest premieres and awards ceremonies, and her cousin always looked in her element, sparkling and dazzling with the best of them.

"Why don't you come too? C'mon, Caitlyn—it would be fun! You could wear your gorgeous new dress..." Pomona urged.

Caitlyn laughed again and shook her head. "No thanks. I'd just be terrified and hiding in the corner. I'm not you, Pomie—I don't know how you do it, going up and talking to total strangers."

"You just smile and say hello," said Pomona. "You've been doing it here in Tillyhenge."

"That's not the same," Caitlyn protested. "It's a lot easier in a sleepy little Cotswold village than at some glamorous celebrity party."

"Not so sleepy, if you ask me," said Pomona darkly. "There've been three murders here in the last couple of weeks. And it seems like every nice guy I meet turns out to be a psycho."

"Matt wasn't a murderer," Caitlyn reminded her. "You were right about that."

"Yeah, but he turned out to be a total loser who uses little girls to protect his own skin! Talk about despicable!" Pomona made a face of disgust. "I'm swearing off men. No more guys for me. Yeah, like those detox programmes where you cut out carbs... I'm going on a detox. A man detox."

Caitlyn hid a smile and wondered how long that would last. She watched as Pomona tossed her monogrammed designer case into the back seat of the convertible and shut the door. They heard voices behind them and turned to see James Fitzroy coming out of the Manor's front entrance, accompanied by Inspector Walsh. The two men shook hands, then the inspector came down the front steps and headed to the nearby police car where a constable was waiting. James saw the girls and strolled over to join them.

"Are the police here again?" asked Pomona. "Omigod, I thought they'd asked every question under the sun already. They were here until midnight after the Garden Party and all day yesterday as well!"

James sighed tiredly. "It's been a long process, but they needed to get statements from everyone involved."

"But Mrs Harris has confessed to everything,

right?" asked Pomona. "She's not still trying to deny that she's the murderer."

"Yes, she has broken down and admitted everything. Well, except for one thing." James frowned.

The two girls looked at him expectantly.

"She says she didn't take the bloodstone ring."

"Huh?" said Pomona. "What do you mean, she didn't take the ring?"

"She says she never touched it—that the keys were the only thing she took. According to her, when she left Mrs Brixton's sitting room, the ring was still there. The police showed her a picture of the ring and she insists that she saw it on Mrs Brixton's desk. In fact, she says that Mrs Brixton was examining it when she arrived."

"But... then how did it disappear?" demanded Pomona.

"Somebody else must have taken it," said Caitlyn suddenly. "Someone who came in after Mrs Harris left."

"Yes." James gave her an approving look. "That's what Inspector Walsh thinks as well. The theft of the ring was not actually connected to the murder— it was simply a coincidence of sorts. Someone must have come into the sitting room and taken advantage of the situation."

"You mean—they saw a dead body on the floor and just, like, ignored it? Didn't report it to the police?" said Pomona. "Who would do that?"

"Somebody who didn't want their presence in the house to be revealed," said Caitlyn. "They knew that the body would be found eventually, so they just got what they wanted and got out again quickly." She looked at James. "Do the police have any idea who it might have been?"

"Not Matt?" said Pomona quickly.

"No, Inspector Walsh thinks it may have been an opportunistic thief," said James. "Someone who came in the back door and happened to see the ring on Mrs Brixton's desk—"

Caitlyn shook her head impatiently. "That's ridiculous! The sitting room is quite a long way from the back door. They can't seriously think someone would sneak in and just *happen* to wander down the hallway to Mrs Brixton's sitting room? And besides, if the person *was* an opportunistic thief, wouldn't he have stolen other things as well? Like her purse? There was nothing else taken, other than the bloodstone ring and the keys, was there?"

"Yeah, it had to be someone who came in specifically for the ring," Pomona agreed. "Didn't Inspector Walsh have this theory that the mysterious dude who asked Amelia to steal the ring came to make a deal with Mrs Brixton? I'll bet that's what happened! He came and found her dead... so he just took the ring and skipped out."

"It might have been a 'she' and not a 'he'," said Caitlyn. "Remember the girl who took the ring into the antique jewellery store?"

"Oh yeah!" said Pomona. "Yeah—there's no way that was just an opportunistic thief! I mean, that was someone who went to the trouble of wearing a red wig—like they were trying to incriminate Caitlyn. Which opportunistic thief would do that?"

"That could simply be put down to coincidence as well," said James. "The thief might have wanted to use a disguise and just happened to pick a red wig. I know, I know, it's very unlikely—I'm just playing devil's advocate..." he said with a laugh, holding his hands up defensively as both girls turned indignant eyes on him. "For what it's worth, I agree with you both and I said as much to the police, but I get the impression that now that the murderer has been apprehended, Inspector Walsh is less interested in following up an incidence of petty theft. After all, the ring itself is not worth a lot of money—it's the kind of thing that people buy all the time at flea markets and in junk shops. Its value is mostly sentimental and... I suppose you could say, mythological." He smiled. "Inspector Walsh is a very pragmatic man with little patience for anything related to the supernatural. He is understandably reluctant to invest police time and resources in a ring of minimal value, no matter how incredible the legends say it is."

"Excuse me, sir, there's a phone call for you," came a voice behind them. They turned to see Amelia standing in the front entrance.

"Thanks," called James. "I'll be along in a

minute."

"Jeez, how come she's still here?" asked Pomona. "I thought you would have fired her already—I mean, she tried to steal your stuff!"

James looked slightly sheepish. "Yes, well... I had a long talk with Amelia. She seems genuinely contrite. Besides, she told me about her sick mother and how she is supporting her..."

Pomona rolled her eyes.

"...anyway, she's on a probationary period to begin with, but I think everyone deserves a second chance, don't you?" He gave them a smile. "If you'll excuse me for a moment, I'll just take this call, then I'll be right back."

"James is too nice and noble," Pomona complained when he had returned to the house and was out of earshot. "People will just, like, take advantage of his kindness and generosity."

"I think he's just very fair... and quick to forgive," said Caitlyn. "But I don't think James Fitzroy is a pushover. There's something about him... a sort of quiet authority..."

"My, we're getting to know Lord Fitzroy quite well, aren't we?" Pomona said with a teasing smile.

Caitlyn blushed and said quickly, "So what's this big party you're going to tonight?"

"It's the premiere of a film by that new Scandinavian director, Sven Jordbro—you know, he's been winning a string of Oscars and awards, and everyone wants to work with him. And his after-parties—they're like *the* place to be seen. You're no one if you're not seen at a Sven Jordbro after-party."

"Are they really that amazing?"

Pomona shrugged. "They're okay. I'm not sure what all the fuss is about. A lot of Hollywood stars will be jetting in, though, so I guess it might be fun... Actually, the only reason I want to go is 'cos I heard that Thane Blackmort might be there!"

"Who?"

"You know—Thane Blackmort, the mysterious billionaire! The papers call him the Black Tycoon, 'cos he always wears black, only drinks black vodka, and flies around in a black private jet."

"Sounds like some kind of weirdo," Caitlyn commented.

"Yeah, but a *really hot* weirdo," said Pomona with a lusty sigh. "Have you seen a picture of him? Omigod, those eyes—I've never seen blue eyes like that! The man is like sex on legs." She gave Caitlyn a grin. "I'm hoping I might get an introduction at the after-party."

"I thought you were going on a man detox," said Caitlyn dryly.

Pomona waved a hand. "Thane Blackmort isn't a mere man—he's a god. I'll make exceptions for gods." She looked suddenly over Caitlyn's shoulder and called, "Well, I guess I'd better be on my way. Thanks for having me to stay."

"It was a pleasure," said James, coming down

the front steps and crossing the gravel driveway to join them again. "I'm sorry to see you leave. I hope you'll be back soon? You know you're welcome to stay at the Manor again, any time."

Pomona grinned at him. "Don't say that—you might regret it." She glanced at Caitlyn, then back at James and winked. "You know what they say: two's company, three's a crowd..."

"I think you need to get on the road now," said Caitlyn pointedly. "You don't want to get caught in the rush-hour traffic."

Pomona tossed her head back and laughed, then said, "Okay, okay... I can take a hint. I'll leave Lord Fitzroy all to you..."

"Th-that's not what I meant!" stammered Caitlyn, red in the face.

Pomona chuckled and walked around to the front passenger seat, then smacked her forehead and said, "Still can't get used to driving on the left of the road!" She walked back around to the other side of the convertible and opened the driver's door.

"Be good!" she said to Caitlyn over her shoulder, giving her another wink.

Then she slid into the driver's seat, gave a jaunty toot of the horn, and drove away. Caitlyn stood and watched her cousin's car disappear down the driveway, very aware of the tall handsome man next to her.

James cleared his throat. "Would you like to take some tea in the conservatory?"

"Oh..." Caitlyn looked at him, suddenly feeling terribly shy and tongue-tied. The thought of sitting alone with James in the cosy conservatory—without Pomona's bubbly presence—seemed very overwhelming all of a sudden. "I... er... maybe I'd better go... I've got... er, some things... I need to do... um..."

"Oh. Well, some other time then," said James politely.

Caitlyn wanted to kick herself. What was wrong with her? Why hadn't she just said "Yes, thank you"? That was what she had really wanted to do, wasn't it?

"Thank you very much for the invitation, though," she added stiffly. "It's... it's very kind of you to offer. Tea in the conservatory sounds lovely. I'm... I'm sorry I won't be able to accept—"

"It's all right." James's grey eyes twinkled. "I don't think it requires a formal RSVP."

The corners of his lips quirked, as if he was trying to hold back a smile, and Caitlyn realised suddenly how ridiculous she had sounded. She giggled, grateful to him for putting her at ease. They settled into a companionable silence as he walked her to her car.

James opened the door for her, waiting courteously until she had settled herself into the driver's seat before shutting the door again.

"I see you didn't go to the wrong side, like Pomona did," he said with a chuckle.

Caitlyn smiled shyly up at him through the open driver's window. "I've driven on the left side before. One benefit of moving around a lot and living in different countries, I guess. I'm sure Pomona will get used to it quickly if she does a lot more driving here."

"Is she planning to come back to Tillyhenge soon?"

"I don't know," said Caitlyn. "I don't think she meant to stay here as long as she has. And once she's in London, she'll probably get so caught up in the shopping and theatres and social life and parties, she'll be too busy to think about coming back much."

"Ah... you might be surprised," said James with a smile. "I used to live in London myself and never thought I'd be happy living in the country, and yet... life surprises you sometimes."

Caitlyn gripped the steering wheel and looked thoughtfully through the windscreen. "Yes, I never thought I'd find myself living in England."

"So you're staying?" he asked swiftly.

Caitlyn hesitated. "For a while, at least."

"Good." Something in his eyes made Caitlyn's pulse quicken, then he added, "The Widow Mags would miss you if you left, I think."

"Uh... yes..." Caitlyn tried to ignore the stab of disappointment. She injected a light note into her voice. "Yes, I suppose she's got used to having me around."

"We all have," he said softly.

Caitlyn looked up at him quickly but his face was in shadow and she couldn't read his expression. He stood back from the car, gave her a nod, and said in a different voice:

"Safe drive back."

She started the car, turned it on the wide driveway, and headed out of the parklands towards the main road. Glancing in the rear-view mirror, she saw the driveway curve away behind her, and standing in front of the Manor house, with an English mastiff and a black kitten at his feet, was a tall, handsome man who never took his eyes off her as she drove away.

CHAPTER TWENTY-FIVE

When Caitlyn got back to *Bewitched by Chocolate*, she was surprised to see that instead of sitting at her customary place behind the shop counter, the Widow Mags was in a corner of the kitchen, fiddling in a bad-tempered manner with a small black screen.

"You've got a new TV!" said Caitlyn.

"Bertha got it," grumbled the Widow Mags. "I told her I don't need one in the kitchen—I'm more than happy with the one I've already got in the bedroom—but, as usual, she won't listen to me. Always thinks she knows best." She flicked the remote control irritably. "Doesn't even turn on, anyway."

"Here, let me try..."

Caitlyn took the remote and, a minute later,

there was a faint *click* and the screen blurred into life. It was showing a news channel and the Widow Mags made another noise of derision.

"Ahh... news... it's always news! And so much of the news is rubbish these days."

"I can change it to another channel—"

"No." The old woman got up. "Don't change it for me. I'm going to pop down to Bertha's place to take her and Evie some of this leftover fudge." She glanced at Caitlyn. "Would you like to come along?"

"I think I'll stay here and enjoy your new TV," said Caitlyn with a smile.

The Widow Mags left the kitchen, still grumbling, whilst Caitlyn leaned against the counter and watched the screen with interest. She wondered if there might be any more coverage of the recent murder. She knew that the police had already given a press conference and that the inquest was to be held next week, but that probably wasn't enough to satisfy the tabloids. In fact, she had been surprised not to see any reporters or photographers around when she had arrived at Huntingdon Manor earlier.

The news, however, seemed to be focusing on the upcoming film premiere and after-party that evening, with the paparazzi already hounding several of the big Hollywood stars who had flown in for the event. The screen showed footage of several celebrities arriving at the airport or their hotels, some waving and smiling, some ducking and trying to cover their faces. Then it cut to a clip of a tall, dark-haired man being escorted to a limousine. He was dressed all in black—a perfectly tailored black suit with a black shirt and a black silk tie—and there was an air of mystery about him. A newsreader's voice spoke over the footage:

"... Another highly anticipated guest expected at the Sven Jordbro premiere after-party is reclusive billionaire, Thane Blackmort, who arrived in his famous black private jet earlier today. He is seen here leaving his hotel for an unknown destination, possibly a lunch date. Mr Blackmort, whose company, Blackmort Enterprises, has been one of the fastest growing companies worldwide in the last year, is rarely seen in public and little is known about the enigmatic businessman..."

The camera jostled close, zooming in to Thane Blackmort, and he turned suddenly, fixing the viewer with piercing blue eyes that seemed too vivid to be real. He raised a hand to his temple—it was a casual gesture and yet there was something menacing about it. Hastily, the camera retreated and, a moment later, the limousine glided away.

Caitlyn sat and stared at the TV, her heart pounding uncomfortably in her chest. The news droned on but she wasn't listening or watching anymore. Instead, she was replaying in her mind's eye that moment when Thane Blackmort had raised his hand. Had she imagined it? No, no, she knew what she had seen. There, gleaming on one of his long fingers, was a distinctive antique ring with an unusual red stone.

The bloodstone ring.

Caitlyn felt like her head was spinning. How had Thane Blackmort got hold of the bloodstone ring? Had he been the one behind the anonymous note to Amelia, the furtive theft after the murder? And was that girl—the one who took the ring to the antique jewellery store—a Blackmort employee?

She refocused on the screen, hoping that there might be more coverage of the premiere party— maybe even a repeat of that clip of Thane Blackmort—so she could get a look at his hands again. She *had* only caught a quick glance the first time. Maybe she was wrong about the ring after all...

The channel, however, had switched to sports news and was now covering the results of the latest races from Royal Ascot. Caitlyn decided to take the opportunity to make herself a cup of tea. She paused in the middle of filling the kettle and realised that she was moving about the kitchen with a familiarity that made it feel like home. In fact, in a way, the Widow Mags's cottage felt more like home than many of the luxury hotels and vacation homes she had lived in.

And the Widow Mags herself? Was it coincidence that the old woman felt so much like "family"?

Caitlyn set the kettle down suddenly as she

realised that she was alone in the cottage. It would be the perfect opportunity to look at the photo album again. Perhaps she would find more clues; perhaps she would find the answers to her questions... Caitlyn abandoned the kitchen and hurried to the Widow Mags's bedroom. She turned the knob and pushed the door open, relieved that it wasn't locked. The hinges creaked loudly and she had to stop herself from throwing a nervous look over her shoulder.

It's fine. The Widow Mags isn't a fast walker—it will take her a while to cross the village to Bertha's cottage, and then she's got to walk back. You've got plenty of time, she told herself.

Caitlyn took a deep breath and stepped into the bedroom. She hurried across to the bedside cabinet and dropped to her knees. In a minute, she had the old photo album out and spread open on her knees. She touched the page lightly with a finger and chanted the spell, amazed at how naturally it came to her already.

"Manifesto clandestina!"

Instantly, the photographs in the album emerged, like forms coming out of a mist. Caitlyn turned the pages impatiently, but was disappointed to find that there were actually fewer pictures than she had expected. Most were of the Widow Mags as a much younger woman, with people Caitlyn didn't recognise, although there was one tall, gangly man, with a lugubrious face and thinning hair, who looked suspiciously familiar. *Surely not... Viktor?* There were several faded gaps in the pages too and Caitlyn wondered if some photos had been removed.

She found the picture she had seen the other day—it took pride of place in the centre of the album—and pored over it again. The little girl, with her vivid red hair and wide hazel eyes... Caitlyn felt a tingle go up her spine. It had to be... it *had* to be her mother...

"What are you doing in here?"

Caitlyn gasped and sprang up, dropping the album on the floor. She turned around guiltily to face the Widow Mags, who was standing in the bedroom doorway. The old woman glowered at her and Caitlyn was unable to meet her eyes.

"I... um..." She swallowed. "I'm sorry. I know I shouldn't be snooping but..." She took a deep breath and burst out, "But I need to know!" She scooped up the album and flipped to the central photograph again, thrusting it out towards the Widow Mags. "That little girl is my mother, isn't she? *Isn't she?*"

The Widow Mags stared at the photo for a long time. Finally, in a voice so low that Caitlyn almost couldn't hear it, she said, "Yes, that's your mother."

"And you... you're my grandmother? And Bertha's my aunt and Evie's my cousin, right?"

The Widow Mags nodded slowly.

"Why didn't you tell me?" Caitlyn demanded.

The Widow Mags sighed heavily and hobbled into

the room. She sat down on the bed but didn't answer. Caitlyn hesitated, then sat down next to her.

"Why didn't you tell me?" she asked again, more softly. "How could you not let me know that you are my family?"

The Widow Mags didn't look at her. "Does it matter?"

"Yes, it matters. It matters a lot to me!" Caitlyn cried passionately. "All my life, I've never felt like I belonged and I could never understand why. My mother—my adoptive mother—was kind to me but there was always a coolness, a distance, between us. I felt guilty because I often used to imagine that I was a lost child, a changeling, from a different family... and now, I find that that dream was true."

"Well, now you know," said the Widow Mags brusquely, getting up from the bed.

Caitlyn stared at her. "Wait... no, you can't just leave it like that! You have to tell me more! Where's my mother? What happened to her? Why did she give me up? YOU HAVE TO TELL ME!"

The Widow Mags whirled around, her hair wild and her eyes blazing, looking suddenly like a witch straight out of a Halloween horror story. Caitlyn hastily snapped her mouth shut and scuttled backwards on the bed.

"I don't *have* to tell you anything," the Widow Mags growled. "I will teach you the craft of becoming a witch; I will train you and guide you and show you how to harness magic to do your bidding... but I will not answer questions. Remember that—if you decide to stay."

She stalked out of the room. Caitlyn stood up slowly from the bed, swallowing her frustration. She was furious at the Widow Mags. Why did she have to be so stubborn?

I'm not going to give up, Caitlyn decided. She wouldn't push things now—instead, she would bide her time and wait for her chance. *You catch more flies with honey than with vinegar*, she reminded herself. She would let the Widow Mags think that she had meekly accepted her rules and impress the old witch with her dedication to her training; she'd be the model granddaughter and make her proud. Then, once the old witch grew to know and love her, surely she would let down her defences and tell Caitlyn everything?

Oh yes, Caitlyn smiled to herself. *The Widow Mags is going to find that her granddaughter can be just as stubborn as she is!*

She was startled out of her thoughts by the sound of a little girl's voice and she recognised it as Molly. Her spirits lifting, Caitlyn hurried out to the shop. She hadn't seen the little girl since the Garden Party two days ago and she was keen to find out if Molly was okay. She stepped out into the shop area to see the little girl facing the Widow Mags across the counter, a shy smile on her face.

"...and which one would you like?" the Widow

Mags was asking, her voice unusually gentle.

"The chocolate lollipop," the little girl whispered. "The one with the smiley face."

The Widow Mags lifted a chocolate lollipop from the jar on the counter and was about to give it to the child when she paused and asked warily:

"Does your mother know that you're here? Maybe she wouldn't be happy for you to eat my chocolates."

The little girl nodded, making her pigtails bob up and down. "Mummy's on her way. I just got here first because I can run faster," she said, adding earnestly, "And I know it's okay to eat the chocolates because you're a good witch!"

"Am I?" The Widow Mags looked slightly stunned.

The little girl nodded eagerly. "You made the magic butterflies scare the bad man away. You saved me—like the fairy princess in the book." She held out a chubby hand. "Can I have my lollipop now, please?"

The Widow Mags handed it to her and Molly beamed. "Thank you!"

She stuck the chocolate smiley face into her mouth, licking it enthusiastically. Caitlyn was relieved to see that Molly seemed none the worse for wear after her frightening experience at the Garden Party. In fact, the child seemed almost proud of her ordeal. Maybe it was because children were so resilient. Or maybe it was because Molly was still at an age where fairy tales could be reality and the appearance of "magic" had somehow turned the whole encounter into a storybook adventure... and of course, there was nothing to fear because in stories evil was always vanquished and the princess always lived happily ever after...

A step sounded on the threshold and they looked up to see a young woman hesitating in the shop doorway. She was dressed in a light cotton shirtdress and had freckles that matched those on Molly's face. Her eyes darted around and she twisted her hands nervously.

"Hi... I'm... I'm Kate Jenkins, Molly's mother," she said. Her eyes fell on her daughter holding the chocolate lollipop. "Oh... can... can I give you some money for that?"

The Widow Mags had stiffened when she saw the younger woman but now she relaxed slightly. She waved a hand. "No, no, it's a gift." She hesitated, then added gruffly, "I hope it was all right to give it to her."

Kate gave an embarrassed smile. "Oh, yes... thank you. Molly's been pestering me ever since the party. She really wanted a chocolate lollipop and she was terribly disappointed when she didn't get one that day."

An awkward silence descended in the store.

Finally, the Widow Mags waved a hand towards the truffles displayed under the counter and said, "Would you like to try some chocolates yourself?"

"Er..." The young woman approached the counter hesitantly. "Actually, I... I came to thank you."

"To *thank* me?"

"Yes. For saving Molly," said Kate Jenkins in a rush. "I saw what you did... with those butterflies. It was... incredible... magical..." She paused, then raised her chin and looked the Widow Mags straight in the eye. "You saved my daughter that day. I'll never be able to thank you enough... I... I don't know if you're really a witch... and I don't care. I'm glad you're a part of this village. I hope... I hope we might be friends?" She held her hand out shyly.

The Widow Mags looked speechless for a moment, then slowly she shook Kate's hand, a flush of pleasure colouring her wrinkled cheeks. She looked away and said gruffly, "Of course, of course... No need to make a hullaballoo about it! Glad to help if I can... Have some of my chocolates!" she ordered, pulling out a tray of truffles from beneath the glass counter and shoving it under the other woman's nose.

Kate looked slightly taken aback at the abrupt command, but she caught Caitlyn's eye, smiled gamely, and picked a truffle from the tray. "Okay... I'll try this one."

Caitlyn watched in anticipation as Kate put the chocolate truffle in her mouth. It was always great fun watching others experience the Widow Mags's mouth-watering chocolates. The other woman chewed, stopped, closed her eyes, and sighed in ecstasy. "Oooh... It's *amazing*! What's in it?"

"That's a mocha truffle," said the Widow Mags proudly. "It's a dark chocolate cup filled with espresso ganache, topped with white chocolate, and sprinkled with dark chocolate shavings."

"Try the salted caramel and Belgian milk chocolate," Caitlyn suggested with a smile, coming forwards to join them. "Or the rum coconut—that's got Malibu rum ganache, wrapped in a swirl of milk and white chocolate, and topped with toasted coconut. It's one of my favourites!"

By the time Kate and Molly finally left *Bewitched by Chocolate*, they had gone through most of the Widow Mags's truffle flavours, five gourmet chocolate bars, several chocolate-dipped strawberries, and a good helping of leftover fudge from the party... and nobody needed dinner anymore.

Caitlyn hummed contentedly as she helped the Widow Mags shut up the shop, smiling to herself as she remembered Kate and Molly's warm company and happy laughter. She knew this was just a small victory—there was still a long way to go in winning the whole village over—but suddenly her heart felt full of hope and cheerfulness.

An old Chinese proverb she had heard on her travels came back to her: *"The journey of a thousand miles begins with a single step."*

Caitlyn glanced at the decadent treats displayed

on the shelves around her and her smile broadened. *And how can you go wrong when you have chocolate to take on the journey?*

FINIS

ACKNOWLEDGMENTS

Thank you once again to my wonderful beta readers: Connie Leap, Basma Alwesh, Jenn Roseton and Melanie G. Howe, for always finding time to fit me into their busy schedules—their thoughtful feedback plays a large part in making this book the best it can be.

And as always, I couldn't do it without my amazing husband, and his constant support and encouragement. He is one man in a million.